FILTHY FICTION

THEIR LITTLE LIAR, BOOK 1

CALISTA JAYNE

Filthy Fiction (Their Little Liar, Book 1)

by Calista Jayne

Copyright 2022 Calista Jayne. All rights reserved.

This book is a work of fiction. All names, characters, places, and incidents are either products of the author's imagination or are used fictitiously. Any resemblance to actual persons, living or dead; events; or settings is entirely coincidental or used fictitiously. This book contains graphic sexual situations. Every character in this book is a consenting adult.

ABOUT THE BOOK

***What do you get when you cross a steamy romance author with two hot guys who compete for her attention?
A whole f-ton of sexual frustration.***

And that's where I find myself, caught between my father's best friend and the man he hires to be my bodyguard.

Each man turns me on.

Each man bosses me around.

Each man makes me want to obey.

It's impossible to choose between them...but what if I don't have to choose?

Filthy Fiction is the first book of four in the Their Little Liar series. It features steamy action with two men who treasure and adore (and might even someday share) one woman. *Filthy Fiction* does not stand alone.

FOREWORD

Filthy Fiction is the first of four books or "seasons" of the series *Their Little Liar*, which was first published as a serial story titled *Daddies' Little Liar* on a reading app.

Filthy Fiction
Dirty Diction
Tempting Tales
Naughty Novels

Together, these books will make up the entire four-season serial.

To my first readers on the app where *Daddies' Little Liar* was originally published: I cannot tell you how much your comments and encouragement have meant throughout the writing of this book! Thank you so much for your support. You've made me laugh and made me want to do better. I'm always striving to give you the stories you want to read.

ONE

Samantha

The cursor blinks on my laptop. The scene I'm working on is underway. Full of potential.

My roommates are still asleep. I haven't had coffee, I haven't eaten yet. I basically just rolled out of bed, powered on my laptop, and sat down on the couch with it. I'm bleary-eyed and tired, but this is when I do my best work—when I'm still half-dreaming.

Taking a deep breath, I begin to type.

"FUCK YES," he said, his cock thick and punishing.

He thrust into her again and again and she welcomed him, welcomed the onslaught. She welcomed the way she would be sore in the morning, remembering this night for good. Forever.

. . .

IT'S JUST a few lines but it gives me the strength to keep going. My shift at the library starts in forty-five minutes. If I type fast, I can finish this final, epic sex scene in *My Ex's Dad* and be on time for work. I'll be uncaffeinated, but that's what the shitty break room coffee machine is for.

The next half-hour passes quickly, in a mad fever of my two characters moaning, thrusting, licking, sucking. They come, and they come hard. She comes multiple times, of course.

And then, the book is done. *Yes.* I punch the air over my head in silent celebration.

I save my work, then save it to my back-up drive, then I email it to myself to save there, too. Paranoid, much? Maybe. But I've been burned too many times by lost work.

I run the story through an error-finding program to get rid of pesky typos, and then through a book formatter. I make sure my pen name is safely in place. Sammie Starr. That's me—or rather, my slutty alter-ego. The cover is ready to go—I paid way too much for it, but it was exactly what this book needed. A woman, blindfolded, faces the viewer. Behind her, a man is gripping the straps of her dress, and it looks as if he's about to rip it off of her. The font treatment is chef's kiss—fucking bright, girly, sexy. I love it.

Everything has come together to create this final

product. I upload the files to my distributor. They are ready to go. People are going to buy this book, a fact which never ceases to amaze and humble me.

Next step, I upload the product to a free book distribution system.

And here comes the part that freaks me out. Every. Single. Time.

But I can't stop doing it, I can't quit. I can't quit *him*.

I grab the option from the pull-down menu. GIFT THIS BOOK.

Then I plug in his email address.

Does he even check this email anymore? I haven't received any "undeliverable" messages, but that doesn't mean he sees these book deliveries.

Using my pen name's email address, I've sent him every single book since I started publishing a year ago. I haven't told him the books are from me. I haven't contacted him in any other way.

And even though this freaks me out, even though it scares the ever-loving shit out of me, it's also the highest of highs. I click *send*, and I'm so exhilarated, I could happily scream.

That would scare the ever-loving shit out of my roommates, though, so I hold back.

Just the idea that Gideon could read this book...

Just the thought that he might guess I wrote it...

Just the fantasy of him stroking his cock to my words...

...does it for me.

The story ended up perfect.

What's not perfect?

Having to go to work while horny.

Samantha

My boss, Izzie, leans forward at the front circulation desk of The Corbin Library. Her curly black hair is pulled back in a half ponytail, which makes her signature giant hoop earrings more visible than usual. The silver glints in the sun streaming through the library's skylight in the lobby. Her wide mouth stretches in a brilliant smile. "Good morning, Samantha! It's your last day before your vacation, woohoo!"

"Woohoo," I echo with less enthusiasm. The woman is entirely too cheery.

She laughs. "Can you walk the new employee through the different rooms of the library?"

"Sure...coffee first?" I say.

Izzie rolls her eyes and chuckles. "Yeah, fine. Were you writing before you came in?"

"You know it."

"And your pen name is..." She raises her eyebrows, waiting.

"It's Cornelius B. You-Don't-Get-To-Know." I wink. "Trust me, you don't wanna know."

"Your lack of trust wounds me," she says.

"Well, your respect is too important to me," I say, "and if you knew the shit I was writing, well...you'd never look at me the same way again. Let's just continue to agree to disagree on this."

She pouts and waves an imperious hand at me. "Fine. Get your coffee, oh writer of smut. And Millie's cleaning the bathrooms right now, but she'll need a tour as soon as you're ready."

If I were still working at the San Esteban School of the Arts university library, I would not be expected to give a tour to the new building cleaner. But soon after leaving SESA, I found a job at The Corbin, a private library. It's closer to my apartment, the hours are better, and despite her constant optimism (or maybe because of it, but you'll never hear me admit it out loud), Izzie is a dream to work with.

After grabbing a cup of coffee, I head toward the restrooms and find a woman with brown hair stepping out of them, a cleaning cart in tow. I don't know why I expected her to be in her twenties, like Izzie and me, but she looks to be in her late forties. I feel odd that I'm going to be giving instructions to someone old enough to be my mother, but I suck it up, because this is my job.

"Hey, welcome to The Corbin," I say.

"Thanks! I'm Millie. You must be Samantha?" She smiles and holds out a hand.

I shake her hand and say, "Yep. Izzie wants me to show you around, so is now a good time?"

She nods and I take her through the main two two floors of the library, pointing out the various collections. The Corbin boasts art and science displays as well as books. Nothing super expensive or prestigious, but as I look at it again through Millie's eyes, it does look kind of impressive, with tables in the center of the rooms covered in glass and housing everything from gemstones and seashells to beaded jewelry and miniature sculptures.

The walls, of course, are lined with books.

I say to Millie, "Each room has a theme of sorts, including an entire room dedicated to the indigenous peoples of North America. Another room is solely about women in STEM."

"Nice," she says.

We move from the room about medieval weaponry, which is very gothic and dark, and into a bright room with paintings of ocean waves and beaches on the walls.

Millie says, "Okay, what's the theme of this room?"

"This is the largest collection of books about surfing—in the entire world," I say.

Millie looks around. "Every book in here? Is about surfing?"

"Yep."

"Amazing." She smiles at the ladder which will slide back and forth along the shelves. "Thank you for sharing all of this with me. I know I'll just be cleaning, but it's nice to know a little more about *what* I'm cleaning, you know?"

"Totally. And the patrons are pretty cool, too. They might ask you about where to find things, so it's good to have a rough understanding of the building."

"For sure. Thanks again."

I leave Millie to her work, and get back to mine. Today, Izzie has me in the basement cataloging a new shipment of weapons history books. The room is well-lit and cool, the work is peaceful and quiet, and my mind wanders while I work. I'm baking up a new outline because now that I've published *My Ex's Dad*, it's time for another story to take shape in my mind, with new characters, new problems, and new sex positions.

My shift is over before I know it, and I stop at the circulation desk to say goodbye to Izzie.

"Hey, have a great time at your friend's wedding," Izzie says. "Which island are you going to, again?"

"Maui," I say.

"Nice. Destination wedding. Bold move," Izzie says. "I hope they're paying your way."

"Yep, no worries there," I say.

They're paying for my flight and hotel, and they offered to cover more than that, but I wouldn't let them. Olivia has made lots of little comments worrying about me being able to afford the trip.

I haven't told her everything about my past yet, but

I can definitely afford it. At least, in theory. Eventually. In two years, I'll turn twenty-five, and then my trust gets handed over to me. I get an allowance, but I haven't touched it. I won't touch it. Keeping my roommates around, publishing my stories, and working the library job has been allowing me to get by and put a little money in the bank each month.

I get back to the apartment. Addison and Greg aren't around—they're probably off somewhere else canoodling. At least now they don't have to hide it from me like they did when I was seeing Greg.

Yeah, they cheated. While all three of us were living together. And they're still seeing each other. Ew. I can't fucking wait to get out of this apartment, but the lease lasts two more months, and I'm not going to eat the loss. They complain about things being "awkward" and there being "tension" but I don't see them eating the loss and moving out early, either.

At any rate, they aren't here right now.

I power on my laptop again and check email. Procrastination. It's glorious. I need to write down the outline I've been tweaking in my head all day, but email suddenly seems much more pressing and doable.

First I check my author name inbox, which is mostly notifications from retailers, saying my book was successfully published. Go, me! Then, still not ready to start on the next story, I check my real-name inbox.

There are two emails at the top, from two men I haven't heard from in years. The most recent is from my uncle, Karl. My mom's brother. He used to come around from time to time and visit with me after my parents died.

The other email is from Gideon. My heart pitter-patters extra fast at the sight of his name, right there, in print. Did he get my story? He emailed me after I sent it to him, so it could be that he's finally calling me out on my fucked up attempts to claim his notice.

Maybe his email is some form of punishment.

I certainly wouldn't mind being punished by Gideon.

A scene begins to play in my mind. Before I'm even aware of it, I'm opening up my writing program and starting a fresh document.

"YOU'RE VERY NAUGHTY," he said, tapping her bare ass cheek with the ruler. Not hard enough to hurt, but hard enough to get her attention.

"Well, I haven't been properly motivated to behave," she responded, arching her back, trying to show him more of her ass, craving that contact between them.

Craving the punishment.

"I don't know what to do with you," he said.

"Punish me, Daddy," she whimpered.

I DELETE "DADDY" and replace it with "Sir." While the concept of calling a bed partner "Daddy" appeals to me on a primal level, I'm not quite ready to explore it in my own writing yet.

"YOU WANT ME TO PUNISH YOU?" he asked in a low, dangerous voice.

She wriggled. She felt so exposed, bent over his desk like this, so vulnerable and open to him. It was degrading, humiliating, and yet it was the biggest turn-on in the world.

"Answer me," he said.

"I—I forgot the question."

"Do you want me to punish you?"

"Maybe?"

He made a tsking sound like he was disappointed. "Oh, babe. You don't know what you're asking for."

Her skirt was bunched up around her hips and her panties were pooled around her feet on the floor. She thought she had a pretty good idea what she was asking for.

"Please, Sir," she said. "I've been so bad. I feel terrible, and only you can help me feel better."

"But it's going to hurt." He tapped the ruler on her ass again. A warning. A promise.

TWO

Samantha

She wriggled again. She wanted it so bad. She wanted his punishment. His attention and notice. She wanted him to be as captivated by her as she was by him.

And as the ruler came down on her ass cheek, her yelp was just as much about pain as it was about pleasure, as much about submission as it was about victory...

I STOP TYPING. I want to keep going, but I still need to read the emails waiting for me. Damn, though. My panties are wet. Thinking about Gideon has always been an inspiration. I could probably get a five thousand-word sex scene out of this particular idea.

I've always processed my life through stories, characters, imaginary dialogue and conflict...especially my feelings for Gideon.

I was ten when I wrote my first story. Gideon Woodhouse had been my guardian for two years by that point. He was mostly hands-off. Kind, but distant. He wasn't a father figure, he insisted. So he hired a woman named Carolina to be my nanny and raise me, essentially. And he stayed in his office and did his own thing, while Carolina took me to and from school, helped me with homework, and taught me to cook and made me help her with chores because she didn't want me to "grow up to be a lazy slouch like other peoples' rich kids."

She was wonderful. I absolutely adored her. She passed away shortly after I started at San Esteban School of the Arts, and I'm still not over her death. I never will be. Losing her was like losing my mother all over again.

But Gideon Woodhouse. Throughout my late childhood and teen years, I remember Gideon Woodhouse in his cold, austere office. He only shared meals with me on holidays, and he rarely spoke to me even on weekends. I almost never saw the guy.

So of course, I was fucking captivated by him.

I wanted to gain his notice. I wanted his attention. My parents had died, and here was this man who'd been friends with them. When I wrote my first story—some crazy nonsense about a vampire and a unicorn that fell in love—instead of sharing it with Carolina, I slid it under Gideon's office door.

He never said a word to me about it, the asshole.

I didn't show him any more of my stories during the remainder of my time with him. Unfortunately, I *did* develop a pretty huge crush on him. Messed up? Yeah, I know. I never wanted to date any of the guys at my fancy private school, or any of the girls. I only wanted Gideon.

I knew he wouldn't go for me when I was under eighteen, but that didn't stop me from trying to gain his notice. I stared at him whenever I could, and I wore my favorite outfits when I knew he would be around. I tried to look amazing. Sexy.

Looking back, I probably came off as desperate and awkward. Wait, did I say *probably*? I mean definitely. I *definitely* came off as desperate and awkward.

However, all that time, from age ten to eighteen, I kept writing stories. And we've come a long, *long* way from unicorns and vampires. At the tender age of fifteen, I started writing smutty, sexy romance.

So, the night before I left for university in San Esteban?

I slipped one last story under his office door. A smutty, sexy romance.

And I never saw him again.

Even now, it stings. His constant, unspoken rejection. The birthday cards he sent while I was in college—

nothing handwritten in them, just my name above the pre-printed "happy birthday" note, followed by his signature. A hefty check included each time, which I always tore up.

But now out of nowhere, he's sent me an email. I didn't even know he had my email address. Sighing, I click on it.

SAMANTHA, I'd like to speak with you in person. I can be in San Esteban on Wednesday or Thursday at your convenience. Please call me or text a time that would work for you.

HIS PHONE NUMBER is listed at the end. No signature. Nothing else. No "hope you're doing well" or "how have you been" or "sorry for being a complete jackass and ignoring you all this time."

"Fuck you, Gideon Woodhouse," I say, flipping off my laptop.

I'm not calling or texting him, no way. Today is Wednesday, and tomorrow, I leave for Hawaii.

The other email, from my uncle, is easier to deal with. He wants to get together for lunch because he'll be in town for a few weeks. I write back, letting him know I'm going to be out of town for a few days for a wedding, but I'll get in touch when I'm back. I'm not super eager to hang out with him because I barely know the guy and he acts like we have some kind of relationship, but he's at least trying.

Unlike Gideon McSternpants Woodhouse.

When I close my internet browser, my writing program is right there waiting behind it, with the paragraphs of fantasy featuring me and Gideon. In the finished product, the two of us will have different names and appearances, different jobs, different living situations and other details. But underneath those not-so-clever disguises, of course those characters will be *us*. Who else could it be?

But I'm pissed. One terse, impersonal email, and I don't want to write about him punishing me anymore. I'd rather close this down and go to a club, maybe Vice, and pick up a bartender for a night of fun.

Tempting.

No. No clubs, no bartenders. No Gideon fanfic.

I have to pack for Hawaii.

Terrence

I'm later than I'd like to be when getting on the plane. The seats are assigned, and Ryder and Jaxon put me in business class. Which is really good, because if I were to sit down next to someone in economy, the passenger would probably weep. I'm the kind of guy nobody wants to sit next to on an airplane. I'm tall and broad and I take up more space than airlines are willing to accommodate in their constant pursuit of profits by way of cramming everyone into seats made for children.

The flight attendant ushers me to my seat and I stop dead in the aisle.

Because in the chair next to mine is someone I know.

She wrinkles her cute little freckled nose at me. "Terrence?"

I take a deep breath. "Hello, Samantha."

"Hi," she says. "Is this your seat? I was all set to spread out."

"Sorry, yeah."

"No worries." She grabs her bag from the aisle seat and tucks it under her chair.

I stow my carry-on in the overhead compartment and finally sit down next to her.

She smells so fucking good. What does she do, bathe in vanilla?

"How've you been?" she asks.

"Fine. You?"

"Fine." She flips up the window shade and looks outside the plane. The only view is of the tarmac and nothing interesting out there is happening.

Is she avoiding conversation with me?

Gone is the flirtatious woman who used to ogle me when I was guarding her friend. I wonder where that flirtatious woman went, but maybe it's best that she's not pursuing me anymore.

Yeah, it's fine. I tell myself I never wanted her attention, anyway.

We danced together once, at Vice. I could've taken it further, but I didn't. Maybe I should have, because damn, she's been living rent-free in my head ever since.

The flight attendants give their spiel about safety and everything, and we're getting ready for take-off. I pop in my earbuds and get ready to do my best to ignore Samantha.

Soon enough, we're in the air. As soon as the seatbelt light turns off, Samantha's getting up. "Excuse me," she says.

"Of course." I unbuckle and stand. There isn't any other way she's getting out of her seat otherwise, because even in the slightly larger business class, I take up a lot of room.

Unless she wants to crawl out over my lap.

I wouldn't object to the feeling of her pressed against me.

After all, I ignored her interest before because I was on the job, guarding her friend. And why I didn't take advantage at Vice that one time? No idea.

She returns from the restrooms and I stand up so she can get into her seat once more. I try not to stare at her pert little ass in those jeans. I wonder what kind of panties she wears. Lacy? Or practical? Bikinis? Or thongs?

"Are you in the wedding party?" she asks, ripping me from my thoughts.

"No."

"I am. Maid of honor. I can't believe my girl's getting married, but at the same time, it feels inevitable."

"Yeah." I wish I'd brought a book—something to hold in front of me to signal that I don't want to chat.

"Is something wrong, T?" she asks.

"Don't call me T."

"Fine. Terrence. But seriously, you're acting like I kicked your dog or something."

"I don't have a dog."

Her voice is soft. "Neither do I."

Those blue eyes stare directly at me. What are we even talking about? Dogs? Why? She's so damn close, I could count the freckles on her nose and cheeks. Her lips are pink and glossy. Is that where the vanilla scent is coming from—her lips? I lean forward, against my will.

Samantha looks startled and leans away.

Fuck.

I shake my head and sit back in my seat. This doesn't have to be awkward, even though my brain is unhelpfully supplying me with images of her lush body against mine, and fantasies of the way her ass would jiggle while I fuck her from behind.

I can't go there. I'm messed up inside, and all I

need to do is resist this sweet little temptress for the duration of my friends' destination wedding.

Samantha

I can't believe I'm sitting next to Terrence Muscles-for-Days Johnson. He's the only guy to come close to getting my heart speeding like Gideon used to.

But of course I'd be seated next to this guy. It's some cruel trick of Olivia's, probably. She pays for my flight and ensures I'm trapped with this stoic, beefy bodybuilder of a man.

He's going to ignore me for the entire flight, I can already tell. Five and a half hours I will be stuck next to this scrumptious giant, breathing in his manly scent. I don't know what kind of cologne he wears, or if that's cologne I'm smelling at all or just his natural scent, but all I can picture right now is me climbing into his lap and resting my head against his shoulder with my face pressed to his neck.

His very muscular, smooth neck.

Since when is a man's neck sexy?

Since right the fuck now, apparently.

I glare at him. How dare he look so good and smell so good and then have the audacity to sit here and keep doing those things—looking good and smelling good.

If this were a romance novel, we'd be enemies-to-lovers and fucking it out in the airplane restroom.

After a couple of minutes, he notices me glaring at him.

"What?" he says.

"You never talked to me," I say. "At least not voluntarily."

His brown eyes are serious. "I was on duty."

"Well, you're not on duty now, are you?" I ask, poking his arm.

He looks down at where my finger has made contact with his skin. I yank my hand away.

"Forget it," I say.

This guy is the biggest stick-in-the-mud I've ever met, and that's saying something, given that I grew up with Gideon Woodhouse as my guardian.

So I lean back in my seat, close my eyes, and fuck him so hard in my head. We're naked, writhing together, our limbs moving in a sweaty tangle, my pussy so full of his cock that I'm gasping from the pleasure of it.

I could write a book about this guy. He could replace Gideon Woodhouse as the stern professor who knows exactly how to discipline the naughty student. His big hands would leave bruises on her hips while he guides her up and down over his length.

Maybe I'd write a whole series about their exploits. Opening my eyes slightly, I peek at him again. Yeah, Terrence could definitely support an entire series.

That jaw—those cheekbones. His intense eyes. Those strong forearms. I want him to throw me over his shoulder and haul me to bed.

I must fall asleep, because when I wake up to the airplane's slow descent, my face is mashed against Terrence's muscular shoulder. I jerk away from him and straighten up in my seat like it didn't happen.

When I risk a glance at him from the corner of my eye, is he holding back a smile?

THREE

Samantha

"Listen up, sweetheart. I'm going to rock your world. I'm going to lick my way down your body and make you come so hard, your legs will shake for days."

Samantha moaned, unable to move. Terrence had tied her arms and legs to the bedposts. She was trapped, unable to escape the scorching path of his tongue over her nipples, past her belly, to her aching, hungry pussy... all while Gideon watched.

I'M WOKEN up far too early by loud knocking on my hotel door.

"Samantha!" Olivia's voice comes through, muffled. "Samantha, wake up and let me in!"

I stumble to the door like a drunk toddler and

struggle to unlock it. It's way too freaking early for... anything. Our flight landed late and the drive to the hotel, shared with none other than Terrence Mixed-Signals Johnson, was tense.

Besides, I think I was having a sex dream. It was like I was writing it out, the scene was right there in front of me, and now it's gone. I think it was a good one, too. Dammit.

"Are you in there?" Olivia asks.

Stupid door lock. It seems to be stuck. "Yeah, I'm trying to open the door. What is it?"

"I need you," she says, her voice urgent.

As soon as I get the lock figured out and open the door, Olivia barrels into my room and grabs me in a massive hug.

"What's the rush?" I ask.

"I missed you!"

Her hug is crushing me. Gasping and laughing, I peel myself away and take a look at my friend. Her brown hair is pulled back in a ponytail and her gray eyes are bright and happy. She's wearing a sundress and the straps of a bikini top peek out the top to tie behind her neck.

"Look," I say, "you look like you're ready to have fun somewhere, but I think I got about two hours of sleep..."

"Sleep is for suckers," she says. "I'm getting married and I want to go to the beach with my friends and fiancés on my last day as a single woman. Experience one last day of freedom."

"Last day of freedom? What is this talk? There's no danger of you being a runaway bride, is there?" I fumble with the latch of my suitcase. If we're going to the beach, I need to get my bathing suit.

"Oh, hell no," she says. "Runaway bride? Is that even real life stuff?"

"I see it all the time in romance novels," I say. "It's a popular trope."

She laughs. "I bet you're an expert in tropes now. How's the writing going? And I don't want to hear about your Great American Novel...the fake one you talk about with your respectable writer friends. I want to know about the smut. Tell me about it while you get ready."

She's the bride. I'm not going to deny her anything today, and I'm just hoping I can do some napping on the beach.

"Well," I say, "I published a new book on Wednesday."

"What are the tropes in it?"

"It's called *My Ex's Dad*." Olivia is the one person who knows my pen name, and I know she'll keep it quiet. "So there's an age gap trope, plus the ex's dad is a total bossy pants, alpha-hole kind of character. I made sure to have a scene with only one bed, because that's a favorite of mine."

"Ha. The bossy pants age gap sounds like Ella's

relationship. You know one of her boyfriends is literally her ex's dad?"

"News to me," I say. "So she's...kinky like you? How many boyfriends does she have?"

"Two." Olivia winks. "Maybe if we can keep you away from the bartenders during this trip, you could find two bossy boyfriends of your own."

"Nope, no thank you," I say. The idea of even one bossy boyfriend turns me on in a major way, but bartenders are safe. I gravitate toward them because they're easy. I can boss *them* around, and set the parameters of the relationship, and they never, ever break my heart.

"You're hopeless," Olivia says. "Come on, let's go to the beach and find you a bartender. If that's what you really want."

"Perfect."

What I want is Gideon. What I want is Terrence.

But the best man for me is a nameless bartender who I will never have to see again.

Terrence

Jaxon and Ryder didn't want a bachelor party. They wanted to chill at the beach with all their friends—including the bride and *her* friends. Which means there's a huge, noisy crowd of us. There are a few people from Ironwood, as many as could be spared from regular duties for time off. Olivia brought her friends—including Ella Marchand and her two boyfriends, Kingston Tyler and Sebastian Crown. And of course, Samantha.

The alcohol is flowing, the women's swimwear is skimpy, and every time I turn around, I see Samantha. There's this twinkle in her blue eyes all the fucking time, like she has some kind of delicious, dirty secret. She's like a fucking pixie. Mischievous. Hot. I had a dark, secret lust for Tinker Bell when I was a horny teenager. Yeah, I'm not proud of it, but just look at her.

And here's Samantha, in a bright green bikini, her blond hair in a high ponytail, and that wicked mouth.

I couldn't escape her on the airplane, but no way in hell will I be trapped by her now.

The beach is large enough, with the hotel bar set up on one end, and another hotel bar not far away. Guests mix and mingle over the sandy area, renting umbrellas and large tents for shade. A couple of hours pass while our group hangs out in a rented tent, alternating chitchat and drinking and wading in the ocean.

I leave the tent and walk toward the bar to order a round for everyone. Samantha catches up with me. She looks a little tipsy, and her lopsided smile is absolutely adorable. The cover-up she wears over her bikini doesn't cover up much at all, and her curves are so distracting, I nearly trip in the sand.

"Hey," she says to me.

"Hi. I'm already ordering for everyone."

"Thanks," she says as we reach the bar.

She doesn't say anything else to me, but flags down the bartender.

"I said I was getting this round," I tell her.

"Again, thanks." She gives me a dismissive smile, before grinning big at the guy behind the bar. He looks like a stereotypical surfer—sandy hair, goofy smile, and ripped.

Okay, I get it. She's flirting with this guy. Fine. She can flirt with whoever she wants to flirt with. I have no claim on her, and I certainly don't want one.

I put in my order while she talks to the guy. After a few minutes of listening to them exchange suggestive conversations, the drinks are finally ready. I give Samantha a nod and gather up the drinks before heading back to our group's rented tent on the sand.

"Terrence!" Olivia shouts. "Thank you!"

"You're welcome." I grin despite the sour taste in my mouth. I didn't like leaving Samantha at the bar.

I pass around drinks. Olivia, Ryder, and Jaxon are all sitting together on a long beach chair. The way the guys look at her, like she's the center of their universe, makes my chest ache. I thought I had that once.

Relationships end. People leave.

Friendships end, too. People die. Cal died.

"Hey, are you doing okay?" Lin Rosewood asks. She works with me at Ironwood, but in the tech division.

"Yeah, I'm fine."

"You keep saying that." She cocks her head, evaluating me. "We all miss him, you know."

"How do you know I was thinking about him?" I ask, frowning at my beer.

She pats my forearm. "I can just tell. I didn't know him very well, we weren't close or anything. But he's missed. He'd freaking love this place, wouldn't he?"

I nod, because he really would. Cal was a bright, happy guy. He was funny. Fun to be around. Always the life of the party. And so good at his job, he died while protecting Olivia.

Fuck. I'm getting choked up again, right in the middle of a fucking *party*.

"I'll be right back," I say, nodding toward the bathroom sign on the outside of the hotel bar.

Lin's look of sympathy nearly undoes me.

The grief shocks me at random times. I fucking miss Cal. It's been months, but I don't know if I'll ever get over it. I don't know if I should. It should've been me who died in that accident, protecting Olivia. It didn't have to be Cal. It could've been me just as easily.

I go into one of the bathrooms and splash cold water on my face. I need to get it together. This weekend is supposed to be about celebrating Olivia, Jaxon, and Ryder. It's about their love and commitment to each other. Cal had his day—he had his funeral. Now it's time to move on.

He would want me to be happy, but sometimes I don't know if I can be that for him.

I'm leaving the restroom when laughter from behind the other restroom door makes me pause.

It's Samantha in there. Her giggle is unmistakable. I've heard her laugh with Olivia so many times when I was guarding Olivia. But right now, her laughter sounds nervous, forced.

"I don't know about that," she says.

"Come on, I promise it'll be good." It's a man's voice. Someone I don't recognize. Fuck. Is she going to hook up with some stranger on this trip, while I have to know about it? I can't fucking stand the idea. I better get the fuck out of this little bar, and back to the beach.

"No," Samantha says. Then again, "No."

My ears perk up and I stop in my tracks.

"C'mon baby," the guy says, "I don't think you really mean that."

Fuck that noise. I knock on the door.

"We're busy in here," the guy says, sounding annoyed.

"Samantha?" I say. "Are you in there?"

There's a scrambling sound, but no response.

"Samantha!" I pound on the door.

"I said I'm *busy*," the guy repeats.

Nope. No way. I yank on the handle, but it doesn't budge. I look down at the flip-flops I'm wearing. This is going to hurt like fuck. But I kick at the door. Once, twice. The wood splinters.

"What the fuck, dude, you're breaking the door!" the guy shouts.

The door swings open.

Samantha's standing behind the bartender, her face blotchy, her blue eyes wide with fear.

"My girlfriend and I were just having some fun," the guy says. "What the fuck is your problem?"

"She's not your girlfriend," I say. "Don't you fucking touch her again. Ever."

The guy scoffs. "Yeah, whatever, she's ugly, anyway."

He takes off to resume his post at the bar.

I want to chase him down, punch his face, punish him for scaring or hurting Samantha.

But I don't, because she takes one look at me and bursts into tears.

FOUR

Samantha

I've never been so relieved and embarrassed in my entire life. I got myself into a bad situation, thinking how dangerous could it be to have a quickie right here on the beach when my friends were close? Little did I guess the bartender would be a fucking *rapist*. He wasn't going to listen to my "no." My bathing suit strap is torn because that stupid fucking asshole yanked on it. And my tears won't stop—they're completely out of my control.

Terrence's dark brown eyes take me in. I expect judgment. Maybe even disdain. Disgust.

Instead, he moves so fast I don't even track it, and his arms are wrapping around me, holding me close. My face is pressed against his very strong, very naked chest. If my brain weren't short-circuiting because of what just happened to me, then I'd be turned on. Unfortunately, I can't enjoy this right now.

"Hey, it's okay," he murmurs, one large hand cupping the back of my head, the other rubbing soft circles over my shoulders. "It's okay. I'm here now."

"I'm s-s-so sorry," I sob. "I was such an i-idiot."

"You have *nothing* to apologize for." He holds me away from him.

I curl my arms in front of my chest. Bracing for judgment.

"Nothing to apologize for," he repeats. "But are you okay? Did he hurt you anywhere?"

I take stock of my body. The back of my shoulder hurts where the bathing suit strap cut into my skin before it snapped. My lips and jaw hurt from where he covered my mouth.

"I'm okay," I say.

Terrence frowns. "But where are you hurting?"

I shrug. "My shoulder where my bathing suit broke. My mouth a little. Nothing bad."

His hands are warm and sure as he looks over my shoulder, skimming my skin, searching for marks. Then he gently cups my chin with one hand and touches my cheeks.

"Where does it hurt?"

"My skin is raw around my mouth and lips," I say. "I tried to pull my head away. He had rough calluses."

My stomach lurches as I remember that detail.

"I'm going to be sick," I say.

When I rush to the toilet, Terrence doesn't leave. He leans over me and rubs my back as I vomit. When I'm done, I realize I'm crying all over again, and my mouth tastes like puke, and my body won't stop shaking.

"Come here," he says, then sits against the wall in the dirty bathroom stall and tugs me into his lap. "I've got you. Just breathe, okay? Slow, deep breaths."

It takes a few minutes, but I pull in deep breath after deep breath, exhaling as slowly as possible. Terrence is doing the same, subtly trying to get me to match my breathing to his. It works. After five minutes or so, I'm calm.

"You don't want to sit here," I whisper. "You should go back to the party."

"You don't know what I want, Samantha, and you don't get to boss me," he says.

He smells like sunblock, salty ocean air, and summer. I want to sit in his lap for hours. Here, I can forget that I was nearly assaulted. Here, I can forget that my life nearly changed in an instant. Here, I can feel safe.

After a few more minutes of just breathing with him, I'm starting to get uncomfortable. His thigh muscles are hard. My ass is getting numb. This floor is linoleum over concrete, I'm guessing, so he can't be any more comfortable than I am.

Reluctantly, I climb off of his lap and stand up. "Thank you," I say.

"You're welcome." He stands, too, and takes my hand. "What do you want to do next? Back to the party? Call the police to report that asshole? Back to the hotel?"

"I should report him," I say, hanging my head.

"You don't have to," he says. "There's no 'should' after what just happened to you."

I shake my head. "I could never forgive myself if he did it to someone else."

"Even if you report it, he probably won't face charges," Terrence says, pursing his lips. "But I fully plan on reporting him to the hotel manager, whether or not you want to be involved. Working in private security has its benefits when it comes to something like this. The hotel will take me seriously. He's going to lose his job today. He just doesn't know it yet."

A flash of vindictive pleasure travels through me. "Good. Do it. He won't get a good referral after this, either, will he?"

"No, he won't. And we'll be sure to give the local PD a head's up, in case it's worth anything here."

"Okay." I take a deep breath. "Thank you. Again. I can't stop saying that. Thank you. But I mean it."

"You're welcome. I mean that, too."

"Can you not tell Olivia, Jaxon, or Ryder about this?" I ask.

His gaze is sharp. "We shouldn't lie to our friends."

"We can tell them after the wedding," I say. "I

don't want to take any of the attention away from them tomorrow. Please."

"Fine." He sighs. "But after the wedding, you'll tell Olivia, okay? You need the support of your friend, just like she needs your support on her wedding day."

Nodding, I go to the sink where I splash water on my face and rinse out my mouth.

"You go back to the party," he says. "I'm going to talk to the hotel manager and then I'll join you."

I shouldn't like it that he's telling me what to do. But right now? I need that direction, that care.

"All right. Thanks again."

He waits until I'm out of the bathroom and safe in the tent before he emerges and walks around the bar toward the hotel.

I find a seat next to Ella, because she's sitting on the other side of the tent, away from Olivia. She doesn't know me as well as Olivia does, so maybe she won't notice that I've been crying.

But I'm not that lucky. My pale complexion means that all of my emotions show easily.

She grabs my hand. "Are you all right?"

"Yeah. My strap broke and I cried over it. Not a big deal, I know, but I like this suit."

Her brown eyes assess me. She's not buying it.

Sighing, I say, "I'll tell you tomorrow, after the wedding. Don't say anything to Olivia—I don't want her worried."

"Okay." Ella stands up, pulling me with her. "Let's

wade in the water. Maybe some snorkeling? I want to see a fish or something."

I wouldn't have expected to like it so much, because swimming isn't my favorite thing, and the very idea of sharks scares the bejeezus out of me, but when Ella and I put on snorkels and swim out into the water, I find the quiet and peace I need to put my mind at ease. Black and yellow fish dart through bright, spiny coral. I think I even spot a sea turtle, but Ella and I can't manage to get close to it.

That's okay, though. Everything is okay.

Terrence is handling the bartender, and I'm safe, and everything's going to work out just fine.

Gideon

If I were ever to get married, I'd probably want a wedding like this one. Beautiful location, a small group of friends and family. Outdoors. Perfect weather.

But I don't imagine I'll ever get married. I never had the impulse. I barely even date.

And yet I'm happy for my friends. Jaxon and Ryder and I go way back. I met them right after they started Ironwood. They wanted some assistance in marketing their business, and Matt's and my firm—well, *my* firm at that point, or more realistically, Samantha's and my firm—was the best there was.

When Samantha left for college, it was Jaxon and Ryder who dragged me out of my grieving stupor, told me to get my shit together. They didn't know what was wrong with me. Hell, I didn't know what was wrong with me. It took me a couple of years to figure out I was missing her. Even if I didn't feel like it, I had to take care of the business. I had to make sure Samantha was cared for, as well.

I'm pretty fucking sure I failed at that through her childhood—I don't think Samantha ever felt or realized the depth of my care. But at least she'll have money. I kept the company going.

This is an intimate wedding. I'm touched that they included me, and seeing the small size of the guest list makes me feel even more honored, and glad that I came.

There can't be more than fifty or sixty chairs lined up in neat rows in front of an archway which is covered in climbing, flowering vines. Jaxon and Ryder stand next to the officiant, wearing cream suits and solemn-yet-happy expressions. They don't smile, exactly, but I can tell they're satisfied.

Once it seems the chairs are full and the guests are all here, a man near the front strums a guitar and begins to sing. A dark-haired woman standing next to him sings along in harmony.

I don't know who

> I was before I met you
> I don't know what
> I'd do if you weren't by my side
> I don't know how
> To navigate my days without you
> I don't know why
> You agreed to be mine
> I don't know when
> I fell in love with you
> But I'd do it all over again
> And again
> I'd do it all over again.

THERE ISN'T a single person in this little crowd who has dry eyes during this song. Fuck, even my eyes are a little wetter than usual.

"It's a beautiful song," the woman next to me whispers.

"Yes, it is," I agree.

"I'm Cora Fenton," she adds. "I'm a friend of theirs. That's Bastian Crown and Ella Marchand. She's also known as Cinderella."

I don't follow music, but I recognize the names. "Ah. I'm Gideon Woodhouse. It's nice to meet you."

"I know who you are, Mr. Woodhouse," she says, flashing her white teeth at me. "I work for Jaxon and Ryder, so my agency has worked with yours in the past. Anyway, Ella and Sebastian don't usually perform at weddings, but if you ever see yourself getting hitched, let me know and I can put in a word for you."

"Thanks," I say, turning my gaze back to the singers.

I'm forty years old. I should probably be settling down one of these days. Finding a partner to spend the rest of my life with. I'm financially secure, I have a big-ass house that seems to echo with every one of my footsteps. I had to disable the large grandfather clock that used to belong to Matt and Cassie, because every tick of its gears reminded me of the seconds passing, of time going by.

When their daughter moved out, everything froze. The house. My mind. My heart.

It was the best thing for her. The best thing for me. I saw the way she looked at me once she reached adolescence, and it wasn't right. If she had come onto me, even at age eighteen, I would've rejected her, because I'm not a monster. I'm not a pedophile. But that rejection would've crushed her. She has a sweet, pure heart.

But she's out of my life now. She didn't even return my email, and my software informed me that she opened it. She "left me on read," as the kids say these days.

And so, surrounded by this beautiful song, watching the sun set over the ocean, smelling the tropical, flowery scent of this magical island, I make a decision.

It's time to move on with my life. Settle down. Start a family. I don't need to live in my castle like some kind of beast, all alone and unloved. I can do something about my loneliness. And I will.

The musicians repeat the song, and the bridal party begins to walk forward. Like everyone else around me, I turn in my seat to watch as the maid of honor and best man walk down the aisle formed by the chairs.

I gape in shock as soon as my gaze lands on the maid of honor.

She is the last person I expected to see here. The girl who haunts my dreams.

She's the real reason I don't date, the real reason I haven't settled down.

Samantha Joy.

My dead friend's daughter.

FIVE

Samantha

In the epilogue of a romance novel, the happy couple (or throuple, in this case), will sometimes have a wedding, or be enjoying their honeymoon, or they'll be having a baby (yikes, no thanks). Sometimes they'll just fuck, which is usually what I write, because hey, when I write a romance, a lot of the fun comes in the form of fucking. Yes, yes, character development, plot shenanigans, blah blah blah. When are they going to mash their reproductive organs together? That's what *I* am most interested in.

But if I were writing Olivia, Jaxon, and Ryder's story as a romance novel, I would give them this wedding as an epilogue. Because it is, in a word, perfect.

Olivia is radiant as she walks up the aisle with her

mother. Her white dress is simple. I don't know why, but when we were dress shopping, I expected her to go for crystal beads and lots of embroidery, maybe a mermaid cut. Something rich and elegant and showy. But this bridal gown is simple and gently flowing, with a sweetheart neckline and some slight flare from the waist. Olivia's hair is piled high in an updo, and her makeup is impeccable, as is mine, thanks to the small army of makeup artists that Olivia hired.

Tears fill my eyes and I begin to worry about my makeup. The artists promised it was cry-proof, so I guess we'll test that promise. I'm just so freaking happy for Olivia. She went through so much. Drama. Physical danger. A broken spirit. A broken heart. And now here she is, walking up to meet her two men in a ceremony to symbolize their love and commitment.

They are together, the three of them. They are whole.

The officiant says a few words about hearts joining and souls rejoicing. The three lovers exchange vows and rings. Olivia kisses Jaxon, and then Ryder. Music swells as they walk back down the aisle, Jaxon on one side of Olivia, Ryder on the other. I follow after them with Terrence as the rest of the wedding guests stand up and begin to mill around.

"That was beautiful," I say, leaning my head on Terrence's arm for a brief second as we walk.

"I didn't know you were such a romantic," he says.

I look up at him. "What do you mean? That was an

objectively beautiful ceremony. It was like something out of a book or a movie. Perfect weather, perfect view, perfect everything. Yes, it was romantic, but—"

"Relax, Samantha," he says. "I wasn't trying to mess with you. It was a beautiful wedding."

With what I hope is a stern expression on my face, I say, "You better not be messing with me."

"Oh yeah?" His brows rise up and his lips tilt upward in a challenging smirk. "What are you going to do about it?"

We're supposed to go do wedding pictures now, and thanks to yesterday's rehearsal, I know where to go. I smile up at Terrence's sexy teasing. He's flirting with me.

Terrence Johnson, Mr. Stick-in-the-Mud, is flirting with *me*.

The faces we pass are a blur. But I nearly trip over my own feet, because one face isn't a blur. Brown hair. Green eyes. Whiskers on his chin and cheeks. There's more gray in those whiskers than there used to be.

Nope. Nope. Nope.

I imagined it.

And when I look in his direction again, he's gone.

I totally imagined it.

"Samantha, are you okay?" Terrence asks.

"Yeah," I say, suddenly breathless. It makes no sense. We're outside. How can it feel like there's no air? "We look great, everything's great. Let's go get our pictures taken."

Gideon

The wedding reception drags on. Again and again, I try to get her attention. I both want it, and I don't. I need to talk to her about her trust, but now isn't the time or place, I suppose.

She should at least want to say hi to me. I know she saw me, earlier.

The dress she wears is a soft pink and hits just above her knees. Her blue eyes are bright as the ocean, and her blond hair is twisted up and curled in some impossible updo. I imagine taking her in my arms and grabbing her hair, listening to the *ping* of hairpins hitting the ground while I completely undo her.

Wrong. Stop. Don't go there.

The thing is, she looks good. And that's why I *don't* want to talk to her. Because I'm a sick pervert when it comes to this girl.

Her first Christmas after she left for college, Samantha didn't come home for the holidays. Carolina, her nanny, had died. I called Samantha, making sure she knew she could come home, but she just said no in a dull voice, and hung up on me.

So I made the trip from Clear Springs to San Esteban to surprise her for Christmas. It was Christmas Eve when I arrived—sometime around nine. I'd gone to her dorms, but a group of students happened past. I asked if they knew Samantha and they did—they said she'd gone to a club downtown. I couldn't get into her building, so I sat on a nearby bench partially hidden by trees and waited.

I was so still that I nearly fell asleep. It wasn't a cold night, so I didn't mind waiting for her. I had a gift for her in my jacket pocket—a necklace that had belonged to her mother. I'd found it in a box of old things that had been packed from Samantha's early childhood home, and I thought she'd want to have it.

A couple of hours passed. I woke myself up by working on projects via my phone while I waited. I was angry that Samantha wasn't returning home to Clear Springs for the holidays, or rather, disappointed, but we didn't have to be alienated from each other. I could make this work. Instead of ignoring her, I could be a true father figure to her.

Laughter reached my ears. Flirtatious giggles. I looked tucked my phone away, got ready to stand up and deliver Samantha's gift.

But she was with a guy. He looked to be about nineteen, her age. Even though it wasn't cold, she had to be chilly in that tiny little dress.

She took his hand and led him around the side of the building, closer to where I sat. They didn't notice me, and I was too gobsmacked by the sight of Samantha—little Samantha—looking like an adult woman.

"My roommate won't want me to bring you up,"

she said to the guy, a note of mischief in her voice. "Let's stay out here for a bit."

I thought of getting up, announcing myself, but I was curious what Samantha planned to do.

She stood on her tiptoes to kiss the guy. The kiss deepened and continued. They were full-on making out in the shadows of the dorms. For fuck's sake, I didn't have time for this. I shouldn't be seeing this. But if I got up now, I'd look like a fucking pervert, watching them from the shadows. So I stayed put. If they looked over, they just might be able to make out my outline. They'd know someone was here, although it was too dark to see any features. It was easier to see Samantha and the guy, though, because they were out in the open. I had the visual advantage.

Samantha began to moan. Soft, high-pitched sounds of need. The guy's arm was moving. His hand had disappeared under her skirt. Fuck me, he was fingering her right here in front of me and her pleasure was turning me on. And that was all kinds of wrong. I wasn't supposed to think of her that way. She was a kid.

Except, she wasn't. She was an adult. I barely knew her when she was a kid—I'd hidden away in my grief and allowed her to do the same. Still, I couldn't—I *shouldn't*—think of her in a sexual way. I was seventeen years older than her. Technically, scientifically, I was old enough to be her father.

But then there was that story Samantha had

written and given to me. Fuck, that story. Was *that* why I was really here? Because she'd gifted me some high-quality, hardcore erotica? Now, I couldn't stay away from her. I couldn't help myself.

This was twisted. *Too* twisted.

Her moans grew louder. "I'm coming," she gasped, and her eyes flew open.

She looked straight at me...and she smiled. My heart pounded. Blood pulsed in my cock with every heartbeat. I was harder than I'd ever been. She was doing this--all of this—while I was sitting there watching.

She didn't know it was me; the shadows made it too dark to see my face. But she knew someone was here.

And she liked it.

She *loved* it.

After she came, she got on her knees and gave the guy head until he came, too. She kissed him on the lips afterward and told him goodnight. He walked away.

I held my breath. She knew I was here. What was she going to do next? I wanted her to come to me even as I knew it was so, so wrong.

She laughed to herself, very quietly, and whispered, "Goodnight, stranger. Hope you enjoyed it. Perv on me again, though, and I'm calling the cops."

Then she unlocked the door to the dormitory and went inside.

Terrence

Samantha was right—this wedding celebration is beautiful. The ceremony was just as perfect as the three newlyweds deserve. They're happy, and they've earned it.

Not that anyone should have to earn happiness. It should be a right for everyone. But after everything those three have gone through, I bet their happiness is that much sweeter.

The reception area is an outdoor venue right next to a sandy beach, with a casual buffet set-up, a dance floor, and live music. The air smells like the ocean, flowers, and good food.

I try to mingle with the other guests, especially the folks from Ironwood. We're already friends. But Samantha is never far from me. At first, I think it's because she's following me.

Then, I realize it's me, following her.

I wasn't even conscious of it. She's chatting with Olivia, Jaxon, and Ryder, congratulating them, telling them how beautiful the wedding was. Then I find myself shaking the men's hands and giving Olivia a hug, doing the same. A few minutes later, Samantha's loading her plate at the buffet table, and there I am, suddenly at her side.

"Dude, you're off duty," Squid mutters next to me at the table.

I pretend not to know what he's talking about. "What?"

He scoffs. "Nice try. You're following Samantha around. Either: one, you want into her pants, or two, you're protecting her. Which is it?"

"Neither. Leave me alone." We're talking too quiet for Samantha to hear us, and I don't want her to.

"Well, you're off duty," he whispers. "If it's the first option and you want her, you should shoot your shot. If you're protecting her, back off—your looming presence is going to keep other guys from shooting *their* shots."

I glare at him. "Guys like you?"

"Maybe," he says, looking her up and down.

I want to shove his face into the shrimp platter and hold it there until he cries for mercy.

Laughing, he says, "Well, from that murderous expression on your face, now I know it's option one, and you want her. Go for it."

I shake my head as he steals a shrimp from my plate and walks away.

Samantha goes around to the other side of the table so that she's facing me. "The answer's yes," she says.

"What?"

"The only reason I can figure out you're following me, is that you want me to write down your name on my dance card."

I laugh. "You don't have a dance card."

"It's a mental dance card. And yes, Terrence Johnson, it is your lucky evening, because I will put you down for the first dance."

Samantha

I wait for a long moment while Terrence stares at me. Crap, did I come on too strong? Of course I did. I always have with this guy, from the very beginning, when Cora, his coworker, had to tell me to back down because he was working.

My face feels hot and I know it's turning red. I blush easily, a tragic side effect of my lack of melatonin.

"Never mind," I blurt. "I'll go—"

His fingers wrap around my wrist, then slide down until he's holding my hand. "Of course I want to be on your dance card," he says. "And *first* on the dance card, no less. I'm honored."

"Really?" I say, my voice a breathy squeak. Not at all the sexy vixen I want to be, but whatever. Terrence is agreeing to dance with me. Heck yeah.

"Really."

"And not just because you feel sorry for me, from earlier?" I say.

"What happened earlier?" Olivia's voice comes from behind me.

Crap. I slowly turn around and paste a smile on my face. "Oh, just, um..."

"Don't lie to me, Samantha Joy." Her gray eyes are suspicious as they search mine.

I give a little shake of my head. "It was nothing. Just a minor altercation with an asshole. I'll tell you all about it after the wedding."

"If you're worried about bringing drama or something," she says, "I can handle it. What I can't handle is my friend bottling up her own problems from some misguided notion that today has to be all about the bride."

She's serious.

"I don't want to upset you," I say. "It can really wait, I swear."

"Terrence," Olivia says, "do you know what she's talking about?"

Next to me, Terrence nods.

"Okay, come here, girlie. Time to spill." Olivia drags me away from Terrence and to a little area off to the side of the outdoor reception area. The sun has set, and the place is mostly lit by fake torches and subtle ground lights.

It takes me a few minutes, but I tell Olivia everything that happened in that restroom. The way he turned aggressive as soon as the bathroom door closed. The way I tried to fight. And the way Terrence barged in so I didn't have to fight for long.

"Terrence saved my ass," I say.

Eyes full of empathetic tears, Olivia says, "He's a good guy. I'm so glad he was there."

"Me, too. I'm going to dance with him in a bit."

"And the bartender is gone? He doesn't work here anymore?"

"I think so."

"Okay," she says. "Tomorrow, I'll follow up and make sure—"

"Let me do that," I say. "Tomorrow, you're going to be living out sex fantasies that are too hot for even me to try to write."

She laughs. "All right, all right. Thank you for telling me, though. Whatever either of us is going through, we should be able to tell each other. No matter what. Shit's going to happen, you know? You're not spoiling my day by telling me about shit that happened to you. I want to be here for you. Always."

I throw my arms around her. "You're my best friend. I'm so freaking happy for you. I love you."

"I love you, too." She squeezes me back, then pulls away. "Go dance with Terrence. Have a blast, okay? And if you need to talk more, you know where to find me. Even if it's the middle of the night."

"Thank you." But no way in hell am I going to interrupt her on her wedding night, of all nights.

It takes me a few minutes to find Terrence, but I recognize the broad sweep of his shoulders in his suit, and his close-cropped black hair.

"Hey there, handsome," I say, tapping his shoulder. "Ready for that dance?"

He's talking to someone, but he turns to the side, a half-smile on his handsome face.

When he turns, I can see the man he was speaking to. I thought I imagined him earlier. But I hadn't. Now he's standing before me. Tall, forbidding. *Forbidden*.

"Samantha?" Gideon's green eyes are searching.

Gideon. My former guardian.

He'd also been my father's business partner. After my parents' deaths, he kept his half of the business, and he's been entrusted with my half until I turn twenty-five.

And here he is. At this wedding.

I grab Terrence's arm, spin around on my heels, and march Terrence onto the dance floor.

SIX

Gideon

Damn it, Samantha will not look at me. She won't talk to me. Every time I get close, she's spinning away, dancing with a group or with that guy I'd been talking to, Terrence, or one of the grooms. I even try to cut in once, but as soon as she sees me approaching, she abruptly leaves the dance floor and makes a beeline for the restrooms.

Does she hate me or something?

She shouldn't *hate* me.

I know she doesn't love me or anything like that—we had a rather cold, remote relationship while she grew up in that house with me in Clear Springs. But we got along okay.

How is Samantha here, though, in Hawaii? I'm still in shock that we're at the same wedding. Apparently, she's good friends with the bride—they must be very good friends, because Samantha's the maid of honor. I had no idea that she had any connection to Olivia, Jaxon, and Ryder, and I hate that I'm so out of touch with her life. I was supposed to be her family, and I failed.

Not for the first time, I'm grateful that I hired Carolina to raise her. At least Samantha had somebody who showed that they cared.

Terrence seems to care. I wish I'd never met the guy. It would be easier if I hadn't been chatting with him about Ironwood and personal security and the like. He seems to be a decent man. But now he's touching Samantha and I want to rip his fingers off.

Deep breaths. I'm not a psychopath. I don't truly want to hurt him. I wish I *was* him. If I were him, I wouldn't be forty years old and lusting after my twenty-three-year-old former ward.

I'm captivated just by watching her dance. She's no longer the kid who grew up in my house. She's a woman. I knew that as soon as I saw her outside the dormitory with that guy, but now I have a better look. Her ass shakes delightfully while she dances, and those legs of hers are long and lean. Her mouth is tilted up at one side, like she's thinking something mischievous and she's just daring me to ask what it is. There's a sensuality to her, and it's not just because I know about all the erotic, filthy scenes that run through her head.

"Care to dance?" a woman says next to me.

"I'd love to," I say, taking her hand.

She's nice-looking, with light brown hair curling attractively over her bare shoulders. Her blue, strapless dress hugs her curves and she grins up at me as we move over the dance floor together.

"I'm Bethany," she says.

"Gideon. Nice to meet you. Are you here for the bride or for one of the grooms?"

"I'm here for Jaxon. He's my cousin. You?"

"I'm friends with the grooms, both of them," I say.

A whirl of pale pink goes by, and I catch Samantha's scent. Cherries and vanilla. I ate black cherry-flavored ice cream by the pint after Samantha left for college, and it took me way too long to realize why.

Once I did, I stopped eating the ice cream.

Where did Samantha go, just now? Dammit, I need to stop ogling her and talk to her.

Bethany taps my shoulder, reclaiming my attention. She offers me a tentative grin. "Where are you from?"

Right. I shouldn't be rude to my dance partner. "Clear Springs. It's a little ways north of San Esteban."

"Oh, you're a California guy." She pushes her lips together in an exaggerated pout. "I live in Chicago. We're star-crossed lovers and we only just met."

I have some reservations about the whole "lovers" bit, but I don't argue because I'm still looking around for Samantha. There. Her pink dress catches the torchlights before I track it beyond the flower arrangements bordering the reception area. Did she just leave the party? With a man? Was it *Terrence*?

Unreasonable jealousy flows through my veins before I tamp it down. She's her own woman. She doesn't belong to me. The weird jealous feeling I have is only because I need to speak with her. The weird jealous feeling is nothing but frustrated disappointment. It'll pass once she and I have a chance to talk.

I can't go look for her now, though. I dutifully sway with Bethany until the end of the song. Then I step back and open my mouth to thank her.

Before I can speak, she holds out her hand again and says, "I need to get away from everyone for a minute, but I'm a little unsteady in these shoes. Come with?"

She seemed steady enough while we were dancing, but okay. I thought I saw Samantha go toward the beach, so I take Bethany's hand and lead her in the same direction. We weave through the flower boxes bordering the reception area and down some steep steps until our shoes meet sand.

"It's so romantic here," Bethany says, looking out over the moonlit waves.

"Yep." I'm not looking at the waves, but at the gentle rise and fall of the beach, searching for Samantha. And her mystery man.

"Weddings turn me on," Bethany whispers, then she takes my hand in hers and places it on her breast.

The fabric of her dress bunches beneath my fingers as she makes my hand squeeze her.

At first, I'm too shocked to move. As I start to yank my hand back, though, she grabs it and holds it to her.

"If you're not interested, you could just say so," she says. "I'm a big girl, I can take it."

"I'm not interested." I pull my hand away as gently as possible and walk back to the party. While I usually can admire a woman who goes after what she wants, this is too much.

I risk a glance over my shoulder and Bethany is just standing there, looking after me with an incredulous expression on her face. I bet she doesn't get turned down often—she's objectively attractive.

But right now, I have only one woman on my mind. Also, now there's sand in my shoes.

I'd thought a destination wedding might be the ideal, but with the sand? And the cousin trying to make me feel her up?

Nope.

I am officially done with this wedding. Samantha obviously doesn't want to speak with me, and there isn't much else for me to do, with the bride and grooms occupied with dancing and mingling.

I find the happy newlyweds to say goodbye. Giving each of them a hug, I say, "Congratulations! Thank you so much for allowing me to celebrate with you."

"I'm really glad you came," Ryder says, while the other two nod.

"Do you, ah, happen to know where the maid of honor went?" I ask.

Olivia cocks her head, giving me a curious look. "No...why do you ask?"

"No reason. Just wanted to have a word. Congratulations again, you three." I turn around and stride away before she can ask me any further questions. I find it disconcerting and, frankly, frustrating that Samantha wouldn't mention me to her close friend.

My flight takes off in the morning, and I'll leave all of these concerns behind. Bury myself in work again. Try to forget the sweet temptation that is Samantha.

Terrence

As soon as I've held Samantha in my arms for a dance, I know we're going to end the night fucking.

I try to ignore this knowledge. I remind myself that nothing is ever a foregone conclusion. Nothing is ever certain. The bullet that went into my leg taught me that. Cal's death taught me that.

So maybe the night *won't* end with me eating her out while I thrust three fingers inside of her, making sure she's nice and ready for me. Maybe the night *won't* end with her legs wrapped around my waist or, better yet, slung over my shoulders while I bury myself in her pussy. Maybe the night *won't* end with that delicious-looking mouth of hers wrapped around my cock.

But maybe it will. And that thought has my skin sparking every time she brushes against me. Every time those pretty blue eyes catch mine.

With every swaying movement on the dance floor, a part of her touches me, and more raunchy fantasies fill my head. If she only knew the stuff I'm capable of... would she run? And if she did, would she want me to chase her?

She leads me to the beach and I follow. This isn't like me. I'm usually the one leading. I know what I want, and I go after it. I get consent, and then I take it. It's a tale as old as anything.

There's more now, though—I want to know about Samantha. Her life. Her likes and dislikes. The things that annoy her. The things that make her melt.

"Do you still work at the university library?" I ask.

She shakes her head and watches the gently crashing waves. "No, I'm working at The Corbin now, part-time."

"The Corbin? Isn't that a museum?"

"Mostly, it's a library," she says, "but we also display artwork and artifacts."

"And that's part time? What else do you do?"

"What makes you think I do something else?" she asks with a little laugh.

I scoff. "I know what the housing prices are in San Esteban. Even if you had, like, six roommates in a two-bedroom apartment, a part-time job isn't going to cut it."

"True," she says. "Maybe I'm an heiress."

"Maybe," I say.

"Maybe I have a FansFirst account and I sell my underwear."

"Maybe." I pretend to leer at her. "But it would be more profitable if you also sold pics of your tits."

"Ha," she says with a smile and an eyeroll.

"What else do you *maybe* do?" I ask.

"Maybe I tell lies for a living."

"You're doing a good job of that now."

Her smile is mischievous. "I know."

When another couple walks onto the beach, Samantha sighs.

"Those people aren't too close," I say. We can't even see them, or they us.

"Too close for what?" She bites her lower lip and looks up at me. "Do you have an exhibitionist streak?"

"That is not my kink," I say, "no. Why—is it yours?"

She shakes her head, but I can't tell if she's denying it as a kink or dismissing the conversation. "Let's go back," she says. "I think I'm done with this party."

"Why?" I ask. I want to hear more about her potential kinks, but I'm not going to push her, especially after what happened to her yesterday with that bartender. "Are you tired?"

She winks. "Not at all."

Aha. She doesn't want to go back because she's tired of me. She wants *more*. Sassy little thing. Maybe ending the night together isn't as far-off of a fantasy as I was trying to tell myself it was.

We wander back toward the wedding reception. I take Samantha's hand to help her over a large step leading back. Once she's up, she doesn't let go of my hand.

"Do you have anything else to do as the maid of honor?" I ask her.

"Nope. How about you as the best man?"

"They didn't need me at all," I say with a chuckle. "They just wanted me to stand up there and look pretty."

"You did an excellent job of that."

She spots Olivia and the two of them exchange a look, with Olivia laughing by the end of it. Those two have always been excellent at wordless communication. It's like they can read each other's minds.

In this instance, though, I can guess what they're "talking" about. Me.

Me and Samantha, specifically.

"What's that about?" I ask, as if I don't already know.

She shrugs. "Nothing."

"You said maybe you tell lies for a living," I whisper, getting closer to her, "but that was a terrible lie."

"Did you get a party favor?" Samantha asks, her eyes twinkling.

"No," I growl. "You're changing the subject."

"Wait here." She rushes off and returns a moment later with two...lollipops?

"What is this?" I say as she hands me one.

She unwraps hers and holds it up so I can get a better look. Inside the lollipop is a cartoon image of a bride with two grooms.

"Is that—" I start to ask.

"We had them custom made. It's an Oliviapop," Samantha says, popping hers into her mouth so only the white stick pokes out. She blinks innocently at me as she makes a show of sucking on the lollipop.

I can't fucking stand it another second. She keeps tempting me, tantalizing me with little touches, with her big blue eyes sparkling up at me in challenge.

"You don't know what I want to do to you," I tell her.

"Show me?"

I can't show her everything, not without a big conversation which will likely scare her off. But I can unleash part of it.

"My bedroom," I say. "Now."

SEVEN

Samantha

I'm surprised Terrence doesn't throw me over his shoulder. He holds my hand tightly as we walk down the hall toward his hotel room, as if he's afraid I'm going to bolt.

No, I'm not going to bolt. I am one thousand percent ready to get naked with this man. With every step, my thighs squeeze together and my pussy gets wetter. I have never been more ready to fuck.

We reach a door and he whirls me around, pressing me against it. I look up to see his face. Fierce brown eyes gaze down at me and his mouth is turned down in a frown.

"Are you unhappy for some reason?" I ask.

He shakes his head and lowers his lips to mine.

Our first kiss. Scorching. His mouth parts my lips

and he forces his tongue into my mouth. The passion between us has been building all evening. Hell, as far as I'm concerned, it's been building since I first laid eyes on him last summer.

Just as quickly as he started kissing me, he stops.

"Consent," he says.

"You have it," I say. "I want to have sex with you."

"I'm going to take you into my room," Terrence says in a hoarse voice.

"Yes," I say.

"I'm going to fuck you. Maybe harder then you're used to."

"I can take it."

"I can get intense," he says, keeping his eyes on mine. There are unspoken words in those deep brown depths.

"Are you worried about scaring me?" I ask.

"Fuck," he growls, burying his face in the crook of my shoulder and inhaling. "I *want* to scare you, Samantha. I want you to run. I want to chase you, catch you."

"And then fuck me," I say.

He nods, his face still buried in my neck.

Desire floods my panties. I like the sound of this. No, I *love* the sound of this.

"Should I try to get away from you?"

"Yes," he says, his breath hot against my skin.

Holy shit, this guy is so turned on—and so am I. I can feel the rigid length of him against my lower stomach as he presses me into the door.

"Do you want this?" he asks.

"Um, *yeah*," I say. "Should I try getting away now?"

He pulls back slightly and shakes his head. "No, not yet. If someone were to see you running for your life in this hallway, and me chasing you...yeah, no."

He's huge, intimidating. He's Black. Things could get dangerous for him very quickly.

"Good point," I say. "So, in your room, then?"

"Yeah." He teases the edge of my sleeve, his fingers rough and warm against my skin. "If it's too much, we don't have to do it."

It's a lot, but it isn't too much. "I've never done this before," I say. "I don't think it's too much, but what if I change my mind?"

"Good question."

His nod of approval turns me on, too. Everything this guy does turns me on. It's not fair.

He says, "You need a safe word. *Red* is a good one, but you can pick whatever you want."

"I'll go with *red*," I say.

His hand is still on my shoulder, teasing the strap of my dress. I lean into his touch.

"I'm asking a lot if this is the first time you've done this," he says. "Especially after what happened yesterday with that bartender."

"That won't bother me, I don't think so, anyway," I say.

"If you say red but you still want to mess around,

we can just fuck without the chase and that'll be fun, too."

"I want to do this," I say.

He nods, grips the back of my neck, and kisses me hard again. "You taste so sweet."

Reaching into his back pocket, he pulls out his hotel key card and unlocks the door. It swings open behind me and suddenly, Terrence is no longer holding me. I feel strangely vulnerable.

His eyes shine with a predatory gleam. "Run, little girl."

I look over my shoulder. There isn't far to go. It's a single room with one queen bed. There's a sliding door that goes out onto a balcony, and a bathroom. He's going to catch me in less than five seconds. Even though the balcony door is open, I'm not going there—we're only on the second floor, but that's too dangerous. I suppose I could run to the bathroom and hope to lock the door before he can push it open—

"Run," Terrence says again.

No time for thinking. No time for planning. I spin around and rush into the room. If I can put the bed between us, maybe I can dodge him that way.

I'm afraid to look behind me, but I risk a glance over my shoulder. He's leisurely following me into the room. I race to the other side of the bed and face him.

He latches the deadbolt and smiles at me. "You're trapped in here with me now."

"Yeah, well, you haven't caught me yet," I say, trying to sound like I don't want him to catch me.

But I do.

The bulge in his pants is thick and heavy-looking, though. This is turning him on. I think he really must like this game, so I can play along a little more.

He *tsk*s and shakes his head. He walks over to the edge of the bed on the far side from me and leans forward.

"Do you think that's going to work?" he asks.

I back up a little. Not too far. I can't tell if he's going to lunge over the top of the bed, or rush around the foot of it. Whichever he picks, I'll be doing the opposite. I'm glad my sandals have low heels. It's too bad I can't just slip them off—they have buckles. I should've thought of that before I rushed over here.

Keeping my eyes on Terrence, I lift one foot and reach down, trying to unbuckle the strap with one hand.

He chuckles. "You don't have time for that, little girl."

The words are no sooner out of his mouth than he's lunging around the foot of the bed, his arms outstretched.

I vault myself over the top of it and scramble across the comforter toward the other side.

His hand locks around my ankle.

I yelp in surprise—how did he grab me so quickly? I thought I was faster. His grip is firm, but I kick backward, hard, and dislodge his grasp. My knees and hands sink into the mattress while I try to crawl across it. Since when did this bed get so big? The other side seems so far away.

A heavy, solid weight lands on top of me. My face presses into the comforter.

"Oof," I say.

His thick cock presses against one of my legs. Damn, he's huge. Like, romance novel hero huge. This is the kind of dick I write about in my books. I wonder if he'll stop for a minute so I can take notes.

The idea makes me giggle.

"You think this is funny?" he asks in a low voice.

"No," I say, sobering as he reaches around me to cup one of my breasts and squeeze.

"Good, because you can't get away now."

I wish I'd been able to run from him for longer, because it seemed like he was into it. But here we are now, and it doesn't seem like either of us is complaining.

He shoves up my dress. I struggle, trying to wiggle away from his legs, which are pinning me down. He slaps my ass, and I feel the sting through my flimsy underwear.

I look over my shoulder at him. "You just—you just spanked me!"

Leaning back slightly, he says, "I'm sorry. I didn't mean to do that. I won't again, if you don't want it."

I've been spanked before, but not so hard, more in a

playful way. The sting of Terrence's spank seems to have shot straight to my pussy, though.

"No, I don't mind. I...I think I liked it."

"Fuck, you're perfect," he says, and spanks me again.

His fingers are rough as he yanks down my underwear. I half-heartedly try to get away, and he growls in frustration.

"If we were at my place, I'd tie you to the bed," he says.

I like the sound of that. I've never wanted to be so wholly at another person's mercy before. This is the stuff of fantasies, right here.

"If you try to get away again, Samantha," he says, "I will spank you hard and it will fucking hurt. Do you understand?"

"Yes, sir," I say.

"*Sir*, huh?" He chuckles. "That'll do."

I want to ask him if there's something else he'd rather I call him. Hell, I'd call him master at this point, or Mr. Johnson, or whatever he wants. But he's yanking my panties down over my hips, and the night breeze coming from the balcony makes me shiver.

His hands are rough as he lifts my hips. The movement presses my face harder into the bed and I have to turn my head so I don't suffocate.

He caresses my ass cheeks. "Don't move. I'm putting on a condom."

He shows the foil square to me. When he pulls it

back, I hear the crinkle of the wrapper ripping. His zipper is loud as he yanks it down. I try to watch—I want to see his cock—but the angle is wrong.

A second later, I feel him at my entrance. Not his cock, though. It's his mouth. I gasp in surprise at the warm wet drag of his tongue over my folds.

"You taste so good," he says, pulling back.

My hips try to follow him of their own accord, my body chasing the pleasure he is so capable of providing.

He chuckles. "Hold still, baby. I'll take care of you."

He continues to eat me out from behind. I've never had a guy go down on me in this position before, and it feels different—I feel more exposed, like I'm wide open for him and unable to control anything. I can't grip his hair to direct his movements, or lift my hips to increase the pressure of his tongue. He is fully in control. And it is *amazing*.

When he presses a finger into my opening and pumps it in and out, I moan loudly.

"Yes, yes, there," I say. "That's perfect, feels so good."

"Louder," he says.

"Yes, sir!" I shout.

"Fuck." He pulls back.

"Why are you stopping?" I ask. If he doesn't come back to me soon, I'm going to fall to the ground at his feet and beg.

"I need to be inside of you and I want you to watch," he says, lifting me up.

I'm not sure if I should try to get away or not. Are we still playing his game? But I don't want to get away. I need him to fuck me. That chase, and then being caught, being overpowered by him...in-fucking-credible.

So I don't try to get away. He leads me over to the dresser and bends me over it. We're facing the mirror. My face is splotchy pink from excitement, my nipples hard points. And Terrence looming behind me—he looks like some kind of punishing god. It's so raw, the naked frustration and need on his face.

"Now?" I ask.

Please let him say yes, please let him say yes. I've been dreaming about this moment for an embarrassing length of time.

"Now," he says, and slams into me.

I cry out in pleasure. I want to weep because this has been so long in coming. He fills me perfectly—almost too tight, and then as we move, I can feel all of him filling all of me, every nerve ending sparking with the contact. He reaches around to grab my breasts, his hands cupping them, pinching my nipples between his fingers.

"Yes," I shout.

Terrence begins fucking me harder. The brutal, punishing rhythm and his angle causes him to hit my g-spot on each stroke. I brace myself on the dresser, but with every thrust of his cock into me, the mirror bangs against the wall. I hope it isn't too loud for whoever is next door, or maybe the room is empty—or maybe the occupants are in there, aware of what Terrence and I are doing in here.

That idea turns me on even more. This floor was reserved for the wedding party, and there were no kids in attendance, so I don't have to worry about scandalizing any children. Besides, the reception was still going strong when Terrence and I left. Chances are, the room is empty.

Doesn't matter. Just the thought of someone being close enough to hear us has me even wetter. Terrence's hands are tight on my hips.

"Watch," he says, his voice hoarse. "Watch in the mirror."

The view is incredible—my body jostled with each of his thrusts, my smaller body framed by his larger one behind me. The mirror is too high for me to see where we join, but that doesn't matter—I can imagine what it looks like, and the way it feels is so arousing I think I'm going to combust.

My lips part and a loud moan comes from my throat. Terrence grins at me in the mirror and adjusts our angle and it feels even better than it did. I moan again, unable to help myself.

Someone knocks on the wall and an irritated male voice calls, "Quiet down!"

I squeak in surprise and helplessly meet Terrence's eyes in the mirror.

"You heard the man." Terrence's hand starts to come up so he can cover my mouth, but he quickly takes it away. "Nearly forgot—sorry."

"It's okay," I pant, and bring his hand up to my mouth. I kiss his palm before placing it over my lips.

My moaning is muffled, my shouts of ecstasy quieter. But the pleasure is just as wild, just as untamed. Someone *is* next door, after all, and Terrence whispers in my ear, "If you aren't quiet, he'll hear us. He'll know what a slutty little girl you are, coming all over my cock, begging me for it. You better be quiet."

My muscles tighten around him and my legs go rigid as I come. If my mouth were free, I'd be screaming out my pleasure, but as it is, my sounds are muffled.

"Fuck, yes," Terrence says, pumping several more times, his frantic movements pulling another orgasm from me. "Fuck—yes."

His arms band around me and he lifts me up in his arms while he comes, my back to his front, my feet leaving the ground. I can watch his cock piston in and out of me until his hips go still and his cock stops moving. I can feel the pulsing of his orgasm, though, and I stare at our reflections, at his upturned face, his eyes squeezed tightly closed while he releases into me.

When he opens his eyes, he gazes at me in wonder. He holds me up while he pulls out. "Come to bed and rest."

He tucks me in and I lie there while he deals with the condom. A minute later, he slides into the sheets next to me.

"That was better than I ever imagined," he says.

"Same," I sigh, snuggling against his shoulder and looking up at his face. "I should get going, though."

Frowning, he says, "Nah, stay the night."

"You sure? I'm leaving in the morning," I say. "You?"

"The next day. Squid, Roman, and I are doing a fishing thing together."

"So we won't be on the same flight," I say.

He shakes his head. There's something in his expression, a closed-off look. During sex, when we'd been watching each other's faces in the mirror, there had been more. He'd been raw and real with me. But now, that version of Terrence is gone.

"This was a one-time thing, wasn't it?" I ask.

He leans back against the pillows and tugs me against him. "Yeah, that's probably for the best."

Probably for the best? Damn, that hurts. I gently try to pull away.

"Where are you going?" he asks.

"Back to my room?"

"Nope, you're staying here for the night. I caught you, and you're mine."

He's claiming me, and yet he's going to toss me aside in the morning? That doesn't sit right with me.

But he's so damn comfortable to lean against, and

he smells so good. I resolve to stay awake and enjoy this, then sneak off when he's asleep.

Samantha

Freaking dammit. I fell asleep, and now it's morning. I'm practically lying across Terrence's naked torso, spread over him like a human blanket. One of his hands rests on my hip, anchoring me to him. Beneath my cheek, his heart beats a steady, relaxing rhythm.

It reminds me of the way my pulse pounded in my ears last night as he caught me and pushed me against the dresser.

My pussy clenches at the memory. I want more. And now I'm pissed because I can't have it. He wants this to be a one-night-stand.

That's it, I'm out of here. Shit, where's my room key?

The weak light guides me to my dress, which lies in a crumpled heap near the dresser and the mirror. Even though I'm sore, I want to climb back into the bed and get him to fuck me again.

But I have a flight to catch, and he said it's a one-time thing, and I have more pride than that.

I find my hotel key card inside my bra next to my dress. So at least I have a way into my room. Sighing in gratitude, I pull on my dress. The pink fabric is wrinkled and I will definitely be doing a walk of shame back to my room. Thankfully, it's early enough I probably won't see anyone.

I pick up my shoes and crack open the door.

One last look over my shoulder at Terrence—the beautiful, sleeping giant. Then I step into the hallway.

I'm not alone, though. Nope. Because fate is too cruel for that.

Stepping out of the room right next to Terrence's is none other than Gideon Woodhouse.

EIGHT

Gideon

I can only stare at the young woman in front of me. Samantha Joy.

"Oh," she gasps.

There's something familiar about that sound. Oh. Ohhhhh. I heard it over and over again last night, at different volumes and pitches.

The reality smashes into me like a fist to the face. *She* is the woman I heard last night.

"That's—that's your room?" she asks, pointing to my door, which is next to the one she just exited. Her cheeks go pink with a blush and she folds her arms over her chest, uncomfortable.

"It is," I say.

"Oh." She blinks slowly, like she's wishing she could disappear.

Something about her discomfort turns me on. Or maybe it's the memory of everything I heard last night. There's a mark on her shoulder. A bite, or a hickey? Her blond hair is down so I can't get a good look.

"You haven't returned my email," I say in an even voice.

"Who even emails anymore?" she asks. "You could've texted."

So now she's being sassy, bratty. I've thrown her off with my presence, and her false bravado is the only defense she has right now.

If not charming, I find it at least a little bit cute.

I fold my arms across my chest, mimicking her posture, but in a way that exudes confidence and authority. "Texting seemed intrusive."

"What's really intrusive is demanding my presence without explaining why."

"I need to talk to you. There are things we need to discuss."

She leans against the wall and puts on a bored expression. "So discuss them."

"Not here. I'll send a car for you when we're both back in California. Are you leaving today?"

"Yeah. But I'm going to be busy. Don't bother with the car or the talk. Send another email or something." She spins around and stalks off, her sex-mussed blond hair shining in the subtle hall lights.

"Samantha," I say.

Not even looking at me over her shoulder, she says, "Bye, Gideon."

I'm tempted to chase her down, press her against the wall, elicit all those same sounds of pleasure from her that serenaded me last night.

Because last night? I hadn't known it was her. And I'd been unable to keep from shoving down my boxers and releasing my dick, taking it in my hand and stroking it to the sounds of her pleasure. I figured there wasn't anything too creepy about it, seeing as how the couple fucking wasn't trying to keep quiet, even after I'd knocked on the wall to alert them that they had a listening audience.

I'd listened hard. I'd pictured them in all sorts of positions. I thought of the woman on her back, her legs out, while the guy fucked her. I thought of him eating her out while her knees were bent, her heels resting on the edge of the bed.

But I hadn't known it was Samantha. Samantha's muffled cries. Samantha's orgasm. Samantha's naked body being pounded against whatever piece of furniture they'd knocked rhythmically against the wall.

Fuck, I want her. I know how her mind works. It would be so fucking good, but it's so fucking *wrong*.

I glance quickly at their hotel door, half expecting Terrence to step out of it. Now that I know it was Samantha, I'm pretty sure she was with Terrence because she left with him last night. He's a lucky bastard. He doesn't come to her with all the baggage I have. He's younger than I am, too, I'm guessing.

Terrence and Samantha—they would make sense.

Me and Samantha? We'd just be wrong on way too many levels.

Terrence

I wake up to an empty bed. Can't say I'm surprised. She'd been ready to bolt last night and I'd had to convince her to stay.

Surprised? No. Disappointed? Very much. It would've been fun to fuck again this morning.

I wouldn't have minded going face to face, to mix things up. I could sit back against the headboard while she rides me.

I only miss her because of the fucking. That's what I tell myself.

I roll over onto my side and inhale, picking up Samantha's vanilla scent from the pillow.

It's probably better she left. This way, there's no awkwardness as I have to kick her out so I can head to the docks for the fishing excursion.

But her pillow smells so damn good. I'm tempted to hold it to my nose and go back to sleep.

I have to get out of this room.

A quick shower and I'm out the door, heading to the water where we're all supposed to meet. A fishing boat bobs next to the dock. Squid and Roman are already here, plus Lin.

"Terrence, you're late!" Roman says, bouncing on the balls of his feet.

"Sorry," I say, taking long strides toward them. "Lin, I didn't know you were coming."

"She threatened to spray Liquid Fart all over the break room if we didn't include her," Squid says.

I point at Lin. "But...you work at Ironwood, too, and you use the break room."

She grins. "I have no sense of smell. Wouldn't bother me in the slightest."

"Welcome aboard," I say.

I've never been pranked with Liquid Fart, but I've seen the reaction videos to pranks on VideYou, so it's not something I'm willing to risk. Besides, having a "guys only" fishing trip is messed up. It wasn't that Lin was purposefully excluded, just no one thought to invite her. If there's ever a next time, I'll make sure she's included from the start.

We fish for a few hours. Squid is the only one who catches anything. I drink beer and try to make small talk, but it's difficult. It hasn't been easy since we lost Cal, but it's not Cal who is distracting me.

My mind keeps returning to Samantha.

Terrence

When I get home on Monday, I step into my empty apartment and go straight to the shower to wash off the airplane and travel scents from my skin. I soap up my cock and it hardens, so I grip it in my fist and begin to stroke.

I imagine having Samantha here in the shower with me, her skin soft and slippery, her nipples hard points as I tease them and pinch them.

I'd bend her over and tell her to grip the edge of the tub, then I'd fuck her from behind. Maybe I'd put a little lube on my fingers and shove them into her ass while my cock thrusts into her pussy.

The fantasy has me coming harder and faster than I expected.

Hell. I don't know how I'm going to get over this girl.

Samantha

I doodle circles in my notebook margin. Then I add a little smiley face to each one. Then I give each one a different hairstyle. Because this is a productive use of my time, right?

Nope. I should be brainstorming titles for my next book. I'm thinking *The Brat and the Bodyguard* has a nice ring to it, but other contenders include *Stolen by the Bodyguard* and *Seducing My Bodyguard*. Maybe I should write a whole freaking series. Up until now, I haven't wanted to try a series. I like getting the story told in a hundred fifty pages and moving on to something new. But with all of these bodyguard titles in my head, could I follow the same couple through danger and dangle a potential HEA over several books, instead of giving the happy ending to them right away?

I don't know. My brain is tired. I've been back in San Esteban for a few days, I'm pretty sure Greg and Addison fucked in my bed and I don't even want to look at them now, and I'm just tired.

Also, I can't get Terrence out of my head. Hence all the bodyguard ideas.

"Samantha, did you eat all my yogurt?" Addison calls from the kitchen.

"Nope, I haven't had any yogurt. Lactose intolerant, remember?"

"Oh, right. You must've had someone over who ate it, then?"

Poor, clueless Addison. I'd feel sorry for her if she hadn't slept with my boyfriend.

"I haven't had any visitors since before I left for Hawaii, and when I do have visitors, they don't eat your yogurt, I promise."

"Well, *someone* ate it," she says, coming into the living room and frowning.

Her straight auburn hair falls around her shoulders

as she looks around the room for the yogurt thief. The dyed streaks she puts in it are fading, the hot pink more of a rosy brown, the blue looking green.

"Have you asked Greg?" I say, opening my laptop and clicking over to Redactible, the social media site I use to waste time these days. It's handy because I can use my pen name, create a group for readers and fans to interact, and communicate directly with people. I haven't checked in for a while and sometimes readers contact me there.

"Of course I haven't asked Greg—he knows not to eat my yogurt," Addison says.

For fuck's sake. I don't know how to help her at this point. Neither of them is entirely trustworthy when it comes to relationships, obviously, as they cheated on me. Either Greg ate the yogurt, or he has a new sidepiece who came over and ate the yogurt. Honestly, I think it's fifty-fifty chances either way.

There's nothing else I can say to Addison. Our lease is up in four months. I plan to get the hell out of here as soon as I can, which is going to suck for them because I've been paying a full half of the rent to have the master bedroom with the en suite bathroom. They're not going to be able to afford a place on their own. I think they know this, but neither of them has brought it up with me.

Resolving to put it from my mind, I click around on Redactible. There are several new posts in the forum dedicated to steamy romance novels, and I interact with a few, respond to a couple of comments.

"Are you even listening to me?" Addison's voice is louder now, like she's incredulous about something.

"Um, no?" I say, not looking up from Redactible. "What's up?"

"The *yogurt*," she says.

Clicking open the message window in Redactible, I say, "I promise you, I have not eaten the yogurt, I have not given the yogurt away, and I do not know who else would have eaten it except for you, Greg, or any guests one of you may have had over."

She slams the fridge door shut and stalks out of the kitchen, back through the living room, and to the bedroom she shares with Greg. He's not home, so the angry muttering I hear is either her talking to herself or talking on the phone.

I start scrolling through my messages. There are some nice ones—readers who say how much they loved *My Ex's Dad*, and readers asking when the audiobook or the translation will be ready. I give them the best estimates I know how to give. Audio and translations are expensive, so I need to know how well the book will do on its own before I can invest in those. Sometimes, it's just not worth it, and I'm not doing well enough at this gig that I can take the loss.

For every four messages from actual nice readers, there's at least one message from a weirdo. There are two who ask very personal questions about my relationship status, which I've intentionally left blank on Redactible. One asks whether I've tried all the positions that I've written about. The other says I have a "beautiful soul," which is nice, but then he follows up to ask if my body matches that beautiful soul, and I peace out of that message box immediately.

I hate leaving things unanswered, but those kinds of messages don't deserve responses.

Addison comes out of her bedroom, her eyes red and her face blotchy from crying. She grabs her purse and leaves the apartment without a goodbye.

I purse my lips. A few months ago, I would've rushed to comfort her. Hell, I would've run to the store and bought her more yogurt, because that's what friends do. But that was before she slept with my boyfriend.

Lucky for me, I'm over it. I didn't love Greg—I'd just loved the idea of finally being in a real relationship. But Addison's and my friendship will never recover.

Now that the apartment is empty, I open up my word processing program and close my eyes.

I start typing.

CALLIOPE DIDN'T NEED A BODYGUARD, and she didn't want a bodyguard. But her dad had gotten into some shit ((figure this out later, Sammie)), and now she stood facing the guy who would be shadowing her to and from work every day.

THIS IS the part where I usually envision Gideon taking the lead role. But right now, it isn't Gideon who pops into my head as the bodyguard in *The Brat and the Bodyguard* (*Working Title*)...it's Terrence.

NINE

Samantha

"But I protect you...and I love you." Alex took a step toward her.

Calliope felt as if she were glowing from the inside out. "You love me?"

"Yes," Alex said. He was close enough to reach out and hold her, but he wasn't touching her. Why wasn't he touching her? She wanted him to hold her so, so badly.

"I...I feel the same," Calliope said. "I love you, too."

He dropped his head. "Which is why this won't work. I can't do my job if there are feelings in the way."

"That doesn't make any sense—"

. . .

MILLIE POPS her head into the library's break room. "Hey, Samantha?"

Noooo, I'm in the flow of the story! What's going to happen next? He's supposed to grab her and kiss her senseless. I start to write about him stepping forward and her inhaling his deep, evergreen scent, when—

"Samantha? Are you busy?"

My fingers pause on the laptop keyboard. Yes, I'm freaking *busy*.

Millie's the new employee at The Corbin, in custodial, who I showed around on her first day. I've barely gotten to know her because soon after I gave her the grand tour, I went off to Olivia's wedding. Millie seems nice, so even though I'd rather not be interrupted on my break, I take a deep breath and smile.

"Hi, what's up?"

"Well, I'm going to get a sandwich at that little deli downtown," she says, blushing. "I'm sorry to bug you. Never mind, I'll just go."

She turns to leave, and nearly runs smack into the doorframe. She's adorably awkward.

"No, tell me what you were going to say," I say. "I need a real break, anyway."

"I was going to see if you wanted company on lunch. Because, well, I guess I do?" She looks down and plays with a strand of her brown hair, twirling it around her fingers. "Sorry, I suck at this. Do you want to grab lunch with me? Or I could just pick something up for you, or maybe you don't like sandwiches, or—"

"Who doesn't like sandwiches?" I exclaim. "Give me just a second, and I'll come with you."

I quickly type a few sentences into the *Brat and the Bodyguard* document to remind me where the scene was going, and hit *save* before emailing the doc to myself. Things are going freaking great in this book. Sometimes that's the case when I first start out. Then, once I hit the forty percent mark, it all goes downhill. Really, I just need the characters to start banging, and things will be golden. Once I get them fucking, they start taking over the story.

I grab my purse and make sure I have my wallet and phone. The deli isn't far, so Millie and I decide to walk.

"How long have you been working at The Corbin?" she asks as we make our way along the sidewalk toward downtown San Esteban.

"A little less than a year," I say. "I was at the SESA library before that."

"Say-suh?"

"S-E-S-A. We pronounce it *say-suh*."

She shakes her head. "I don't know what that is."

"San Esteban School of the Arts?" I say. "Are you new to the area?"

"I'm new," she says with a little laugh. "I moved here from Washington."

"Oh, okay. Well, SESA is a really cool place, and if you're new, you should check out some of the art exhibits. The theater also has something going on all the time, and the concert hall. It's cheaper to attend those things than, like, going to the opera house downtown." I realize that I'm making some assumptions based on her job, and yeah, her clothes, which are clean but not the highest quality, so I add, "If you're on a budget. If you're not, then the opera house is unmissable."

Laughing a little, she says, "I'll need the budget option. I'm guessing you don't."

"No, I am also on a budget," I say. What a weird comment for her to make. Money talk makes me uncomfortable, because technically I have access to it, even though I haven't touched Gideon's "allowance" checks or his gifts. Sometimes I feel like a poser in the "poor college student" sector. I don't tell people I have a trust fund because I don't want them to look at me differently. Hell, I haven't even told Olivia about it.

Millie and I order our lunch. She orders the cheapest sandwich on the menu, so I do, too. But I also get fries and offer to share them with her. We chat about random stuff—the weather, The Corbin, libraries in general. I don't offer any information about my side gig as an author, because that information is reserved for when one, I know someone better and two, I can trust they won't hassle me for my pen name, which I am definitely *not* sharing.

But Millie is funny and warm. Now that her initial awkwardness is out of the way, I feel really comfortable and our lunch break passes so quickly, we have to speed-walk back to The Corbin.

All in all, it's an enjoyable excursion, and I don't even mind that I'll have to stay up a little later than usual tonight to get my words written.

Gideon

I lean back in the car, closing my eyes against the late afternoon sun's glare from my tablet. Thankfully, car sickness has never been an issue for me, so during the drive from Clear Springs to San Esteban, I can work.

WJ Marketing, my firm, never sleeps. We have clients at all levels of success, and for each level, we're trying to boost them up to the next one. Just starting out? We'll have you comfortably in the black in no time. Your company is only bringing in six figures a year and you have two employees? We'll get you up to seven figures. Your company is at seven figs? We'll bring you up to eight. It's what we do. We work with *everyone*, and that was the dream Matt and I hatched and then enacted.

It's exhausting for me, though, that my company never sleeps. We have clients from all over the world, and offices all over the world. There is always someone who needs my input or advice or decision about something.

That's how it was when Samantha was growing up, and that's how it is now.

I pick up my tablet again. Not to work, though—I need a break. So I click over to my reading app. My library has a few books in it, and they're all written by the same author: Sammie Starr.

I click one open at random. *An Apple a Day to Keep the Doctor in Play*. This is a fun one. The authoritative doctor has to convince his sexy female patient to do aggressive physical therapy for a sprained ankle. In the real world, his methods would get him in major trouble with any kind of ethics board or whatever they do in the medical field. But as a fantasy? It's fucking hot. The positions the couple get into make me glad I've kept in shape, because I'd love to meet someone adventurous enough to try those out with me.

Someone who maybe doesn't cheat on me and then disappear.

At least, I think Ashley was cheating on me. I never got to ask her. Which was probably for the best, because otherwise that might have been a very messy break-up.

I don't want to think about Ashley, though, not when I'm midway through *Apple a Day*. The doctor full-on picking up the woman and eating her out while her hips are locked over his shoulders—now *that* is where I'd rather spend my mental energy.

Is that even possible?

. . .

DR. KNOX'S tongue speared her, and she couldn't help but moan. There was nowhere for her to go—she was trapped here, locked against his body. Her head dangled, but she wasn't close enough to give him head. Besides that, he was still wearing his scrubs.

His cock was hard, jutting out against the thin fabric. Melissa cupped her free hand over the length and rubbed him up and down. He groaned against her pussy. The messy sounds of him licking and sucking at her were obscenely loud in the exam room, and she feared someone would overhear them.

I LIKE the story more once they move it from the exam room to the bedroom, other than this one element—the voyeurism potential. I shouldn't love the idea of watching so much, but a scene like this one immediately makes me think of watching Samantha and that guy outside of her college dormitory.

My cock is stiff in my pants. I'm wearing jeans and a t-shirt instead of a suit today because of this trip to San Esteban. I'm taking a day off, so I can talk to Samantha, maybe talk some sense into her.

"We're fifteen minutes out," my driver, Clay, says through the intercom.

I lower the privacy screen, since I'm not going to start working now, and watch as Clay navigates us through San Esteban. I never loved this city like some people do. It's too busy, too crowded. Clear Springs is more my speed—it's a medium-sized city and my home is some distance out of town. I like the quiet and the privacy.

A woman walks on the sidewalk up ahead, moving away from us. She's carrying a purse and a messenger bag large enough to hold a laptop. Her blond hair is tied back in a ponytail and she has on a flowy little skirt and tight top. I'd recognize her body in a line-up, which means I've thought about it too damn much and probably means I'm going straight to hell.

"Hold on, that's her, right there," I say to Clay. "Up there on the right. Pull over."

He pulls up next to Samantha, in a loading zone in front of an apartment complex.

I roll down my window. "Sam!"

She jumps, startled, then whirls around, her ponytail whipping behind her. "What are you doing here?"

"I told you I'd come talk to you this week."

"You said you'd send a car. I told you to email."

I shrug. "Well, get in. I'm here now, let's chat. I'll give you a ride to wherever you're going."

Her eyes are hidden behind sunglasses so I can't see her full expression, other than her lips, which are pushed into a frown. "No. Whatever you have to say can be said in an email."

"This is important," I say.

"You're some kind of stalker, aren't you?" she says. "You know, people write romances about that? Dark romances. But I've never seen the appeal. Stalkers are just creepers, and that's what you are."

Before I can respond, she steps away from the car and starts walking off, her skirt flouncing with each step.

The fuck? I jump out of the car and take long strides after her. When I catch up and get right in front of her, she's forced to stop.

"What, Gideon?" she asks.

"Get in the car, Samantha."

"Or what, you'll spank me? You're not my dad."

"Samantha Marie Joy, get into that car right fucking now."

She gives me a bitter laugh. "Bringing out the middle name, huh? Like a *parent*? You don't get that privilege. Fuck you."

"I will keep following you. I'll email. I'll text. I'll come down and wait in front of your house. This is serious, Samantha. We really need to talk. I'd rather do it now than waste a bunch of our time. I can tell you hate me, so we'll just get this over with as fast as possible, right here, right now."

She seems to consider me for a long moment before nodding once. Without a word, she stalks past me, back toward the car, and she climbs in.

Technically, this is a victory. Why does it feel like a loss?

TEN

Samantha

I can't believe I'm riding in the back of Gideon's car. I almost feel like a teenager again, sitting back here. The leather is cool against the back of my bare thighs. The interior smells like Gideon—woodsmoke, like the fireplace in his home office. I could hear it crackling away in the winters when I'd hover near the closed door.

Clay is in the driver's seat. He's a decade older than Gideon, so entering his fifties soon, if he hasn't already had his birthday. He sometimes gave me rides to and from school when Carolina wasn't working. I give Clay a little wave, and he smiles with his eyes at me before Gideon raises the privacy screen.

I arrange my laptop bag and purse on the floor, then buckle up and turn to stare at Gideon. Those green eyes of his are beautiful. So beautiful. I've never told him that, although there are a fair few heroes in my books with "indescribably green eyes" and "moss-green eyes" and "eyes so green they make Ireland weep." That last line was too cheesy and I rewrote it before I published the book, but the sentiment has remained with me.

I have a thing for green-eyed heroes, and we can blame Gideon for that.

I wonder if he's recognized any of them, in those books I send to him? I wonder if he's ever downloaded or opened any of those books. Probably not. He probably thought they were spam and deleted the emails without even looking.

Right now, I hope he deleted them.

I squirm against the car's leather, suddenly uncomfortable.

Stubble decorates his jaw. There's usually a little on his face at all times, but the whiskers are longer now, like he hasn't shaved in a couple of days. Maybe he's growing a beard. That would be hot. But anything he does is hot.

I hate him for that. I hate his green eyes and I hate his hotness, and I hate that he's been unreachable for all these years.

"What the hell do you want with me?" I ask. "What's so important you had to chase me down and—and accost me on the sidewalk?"

"I didn't accost you," he says.

Even his stupid voice is hot, all deep and growly. Freaking hell, I hate this guy.

The car starts forward.

"Where are you taking me?" I ask.

"First, to your apartment, where I hope you'll pack a few things. Then, I'd prefer to take you back to Clear Springs where I know you'll be safe."

"Safe from what? And didn't you say this was just a conversation, and we'd get it out of the way and be done?"

"Karl's back in the area," he all but growls.

If I wrote wolf shifter romance, all the heroes would sound like him. They'd all have his impossibly green eyes, too, the bastards.

"Karl," he repeats. He's staring at me, waiting for my response.

"Yeah, I know," I say. "He wants to grab lunch with me or something. He's safe—he's my uncle."

"You really shouldn't meet him." Gideon's jaw looks tight and those gorgeous green eyes become steely.

I shake my head. "You're worried about Uncle Karl?"

"Sam, he doesn't have good intentions."

Sam. He's the only person to call me Sam. Carolina used to, but she's gone now, and damn, that hurts.

"You keep saying that about Uncle Karl," I say, "but I've never seen any evidence or proof that he has bad intentions. He just wants to be my uncle. You're trying to deprive me of the only family I have left."

"I would *never* do that," Gideon says heatedly. "Never. But he wants to use you, Samantha. He wants your money. That's all he's ever wanted."

"Shut up. I think I can figure these things out for myself."

"You make good decisions, you're saying?"

Folding my arms across my chest, I turn in my seat so I'm angled toward him. "Yeah, I do."

"Like one-night-stands in hotels with thin walls, where the occupants next door can hear every minute of your encounters?"

I walked right into that. Even though my cheeks grow hot with what must be an epic blush, I put on a brave face and say, "There was nothing ill-advised about that one-night-stand."

His eyes narrow. "I heard *everything*, Sam."

This whole act of his is really starting to piss me off. My blood pumps hot and fast through my veins, and I'm seized by a recklessness I don't recognize in myself.

"You heard everything?" I ask, blinking innocently at him. "Seriously, everything?"

"Yes," he says, frowning.

"Every pump of his cock, filling my pussy?"

"What-what the hell?" He leans back, eyes wide in

shock. He looks scandalized but intrigued.

"Every pinch of his fingers on my nipples?" I ask, trying to tamp down the arousal that flares through me. "Every time he licked my clit? Did you hear the way he bent me over the dresser and took me from behind?"

"What are you doing?" Anger flashes across his face—anger, and arousal.

I give him a wicked smile. I think I like pushing his buttons. "How about when he ate me out from behind? That position was a first for me. He tongued my clit and fingered me so good."

Gideon's bulge is very evident at the front of his jeans. He isn't immune to this—he's turned on.

"Samantha," he says in a low voice, "you are playing a very...dangerous...game."

"Am I?" I glance toward the raised privacy screen, making sure Clay won't see what I'm about to do. Then I trace a line from my knee to my inner thigh. The skirt I'm wearing makes the movement easy.

Gideon looks from my face, down to my leg. "You wouldn't."

He's such a bossy asshole. What does he know about what I would or wouldn't do? What does he even know about me? Nothing. He ignored me for years. I move my finger higher, daring him to make me stop.

He doesn't move, only watches. Disbelief and hope war on his face. He wants this, but he doesn't want to want this.

Well, I can't hardly blame him. He was supposed

to be set up as a father figure for me, long ago. Of course this seems wrong, even if the whole "father" thing never took.

I bite back my smile and hitch my dress up along with my hand. I pull one of my legs onto the seat, sitting sideways with my legs open. My fingertips graze the gusset of my panties. This is the riskiest, scariest, and most arousing thing I've ever done.

Gideon's hands are balled into fists, resting on his thighs. The car is moving toward my apartment, which isn't far away. If I go too slow, if we're interrupted, this absolutely bonkers moment with Gideon will be lost forever.

Our breaths are loud in the back of the car—I can hear us both over the purr of the motor.

He closes his eyes as if he's being tortured.

For some reason, that gives me courage.

"You can't watch?" I ask, taunting him. I can't believe I'm doing this, yet here I am. "You have to look away because little Samantha Marie Joy is touching herself in your back seat?"

He opens his eyes, looks at my spread legs, and groans. "What are you doing to me?"

My breath catches in my throat. It's the closest he's come to verbally admitting he feels even a smidgeon of what I'm feeling.

"I'm showing you what you've missed out on the past five years," I whisper, then slide my panties aside to reveal my pussy. "What are you going to do about it?"

Instead of jerking away, averting his gaze, trying to pretend I'm not about to finger myself in his car, he leans toward me.

"All this time," he whispers, "all this time you've been pushing, pushing, pushing…now I'm finally going over the edge. Let's hope you don't regret it, precious girl. Make it good. If I'm going to hell, I may as well enjoy it."

My fingers are right there, against my slippery folds, but I pause. He wants this. He *wants* this? Fuck. I'd half expected him to tell Clay to pull over so he could kick me out of the car. But he wants this. What if I'm no good? He said to make it good. But I've never gotten myself off in front of someone before. Not on display like this, not so lewdly.

Gideon watches me, waiting.

I falter.

This is a dream come true, but self-consciousness is about to end it all.

As if sensing my hesitance, he nods and closes his eyes. "It's okay, Samantha. You can cover up. We'll pretend it didn't happen. We won't talk about it again."

I reach over and grab his hand. He doesn't hold back, but I move slowly and place his palm against my bare thigh. Then, as I'd done with my fingers, I slide it up my leg toward my center.

He raises his eyebrows. "I want this so fucking bad. Fuck. I can't do this—you're—you're—"

"I'm a woman who has wanted you for a long time," I say, softly as possible.

He sucks in a breath and slides his hand back to my knee. "You're so goddamn beautiful. Show me your pussy, show me how much you want this. You want it? *You* do it. *Show me.*"

I want it so, so bad. And I can't lose this chance with him.

I hold his hand on my knee and meet his gaze. My breath comes heavily as I slide my hand away from his. If he stops touching me, I won't be able to go through with this.

He leaves his hand there on my knee. His palm is warm, lightly callused. It's a man's hand, not a boy's, not mine. It reminds me of Terrence, actually, although this situation is completely different from the hotel room in Hawaii.

With my heart in my throat, I rub my fingers lightly over my pussy. Everything is slick and hot. I feel swollen and ripe for plucking, like the lightest touch on my clit is going to set me off.

Gideon's gaze is heavy on me. He looks from my pussy to my face and back again. "Touch yourself," he says, his voice rough. "Get yourself off. Show me."

I glance out the window. We're close to my apartment building. I have to do this fast. If we had time, I'd yank down my shirt and let him see my breasts, which guys usually can't get enough of. But I need to come. Once I come, there's no pretending, no going back. We'll have shared this.

So I run my fingertips over my folds, gathering moisture before rubbing it over my clit. Gideon's hand flexes on my knee, that heavy touch commanding me to keep going.

My breathing is louder than it was a moment ago. I'm pretty sure a flush is forming over my neck and chest. Gideon's confident gaze flicks back and forth between my face and my pussy, his attention bold and electrifying.

Feeling shameless and filthy, I dip a finger into my pussy, gathering more of my desire, before sliding it up again. This time, when I rub my clit, I come with a gasp. Pleasure pulses from my center outward in time with my racing heartbeat. For a long moment, suspended in time, I can't move.

Gideon doesn't move, either. His eyes are intent on mine as I take my hand away from my pussy.

"There," I whisper. My legs are trembling, my heart is trip-tripping away in my chest. I can't believe this just happened. "I showed you. What happens next?"

His lips part and he leans forward. Is he going to kiss me? I want that more than anything.

But we reach my apartment building and Clay pulls the car to a stop.

Gideon sits back again. "Now, we go up to your

apartment and you pack a bag. You're coming back home to Clear Springs with me."

All business. He's back to being my stoic guardian and I'm the nuisance ward.

ELEVEN

Terrence

Roman and I drop off our client, Hank Farlan, at his apartment building. He gives us a goofy grin and a peace sign as he heads through the doors, and Roman and I both lean back in our seats.

"That dude's exhausting," Roman says.

"Tell me about it." I pause. "No, don't actually tell me about it."

He laughs. One of Farlan's more annoying habits is purposefully taking cliched phrases and expressions literally. If I said *tell me about it* to Farlan, he would launch into a speech all about it, whatever "it" is.

Farlan's a nice enough guy, though. He needs guarding because he spoke up about human rights on PhotoGram and Redactible, and it earned him a slew of new enemies, a bunch of assholes who've been threatening violence. To be on the safe side, he has Ironwood bodyguards escort him to public functions that have low security, like today's celebrity baseball game benefiting some charity or another.

I steer the company car back toward Ironwood, where Roman and I will split ways and go home after this shift.

"So, you and Samantha, huh?" he says.

I shoot him a sidelong look. "Who told you?"

"You just did," he says with a laugh. "I guessed. Saw you two dancing at the reception."

"Well, it's not a thing," I say.

"That's too bad." He gives an exaggerated sigh, then brightens. "Well, maybe it's good news for Squid. I think he was interested."

The flame of anger I feel surprises me, and I don't have time to bite back my words. "He better not fucking touch her."

Roman grins. "I thought it wasn't a thing?"

"Shut up. She and I enjoyed each other's company. Now it's over." We reach the Ironwood parking garage and go inside the office to make our brief and thankfully uncomplicated report about our shift with Farlan. Then it's back to the parking garage so we can leave.

"Call her," Roman says. "It doesn't have to be over, you know? She's hot, she's friendly, she's smart. You need some happiness in your life, T."

"Thanks, Mom."

"Anytime." He punches me in the shoulder. "Call her."

The duplex I rent is on the outskirts of Old Thirty-Three, a district with big trees and aging residents. Nobody here is rich, but everyone is better off than the folks in Bellefleur. Solidly middle class.

I go inside, grab a beer from the fridge, and sit down on the couch. I pull up my contacts list on my phone. My finger hovers over Samantha's name. I got her phone number when I was protecting Olivia, then never deleted it. I could call her, send her a text. I haven't been able to get her out of my mind since the wedding, that's the damn truth, and it sucks because I don't want a relationship. I don't even want something casual. One-night-stands keep people from catching feelings…or that's how it should be.

That's not what happened here.

She's strong. She's beautiful. Hot, friendly, and smart, too, like Roman pointed out. Fucking Roman has no business noticing these things about her.

Maybe I should text her. Maybe it's time to, I don't know, move on. Try to be happy, maybe. Or at least not so moody. I know I'm no fun anymore.

Before I can make up my mind, my phone rings. The name on the screen is Abe Ramirez. I haven't heard from him in years. No idea why he'd be calling. We used to work together, but that was long ago. Still, because we go way back, I answer rather than let his call go to voicemail.

"Abe," I say. "What's up?"

"Terrence, man." His tone is heavy. "Val died."

It takes a moment for the news to sink in. "Val Braggno?"

"Yeah. He was on the job, and someone shot him."

"That's horrible." I don't know what else to say. It is horrible. "Is the company paying benefits to his family?"

"Yeah, they'll be taken care of." Abe sighs. "Anyway, there's a funeral on Saturday. I'm in the middle of a job in Montana, so I can't make it. Are you still in Cali?"

"Yeah."

"Damn. All the way across the country. Well, if you're available, I'm sure everyone else from the team would be happy to see you."

"I'll think about it," I say.

"Okay, man. Take care."

"You, too."

Random visions of the past float through my mind after Abe and I hang up. Val was a good guy, always quick with a joke, always up for grabbing a beer or heading to the field to kick around a soccer ball. It seems entirely wrong that Val would be dead now. Impossible.

But I would've thought the same for Cal, so I guess it's not quite as impossible as it should be.

Before I can think too hard about it, I pull up the

internet browser on my phone and type in *flights to New York*.

But then I think about Cal's funeral, and death in general, and how fucking fleeting everything is.

I can't. I can't deal with any more death.

I close the browser before I can book a flight.

I'm a piece of shit for not going to Val's funeral, but he's dead and gone. He's not going to notice I'm missing.

Samantha

Gideon doesn't say a word as we climb out of the car. I desperately need him to speak. I need his reassurance. I need some kind of signal that what I did—getting myself off in front of him—wasn't the stupidest thing ever.

But as we go up to my second-floor apartment unit, he's silent.

I need to get into the bathroom and splash some cold water on my face.

And wash my hands. Because I was just...ugh. I was just fingering myself.

In front of Gideon.

"I really don't think I should go back to Clear Springs," I say. "I have a job here in San Esteban."

"Take some time off," he says.

"I just did—to go to Olivia's wedding."

His voice is low. "How could I forget?"

Now he's making fun of me, bringing that up yet again. And after I wanked while he watched in the car, he probably thinks I'm some kind of exhibitionist. Maybe I am. But that doesn't mean I want Gideon Sternface Woodhouse to know.

We've reached my apartment door, but I hold off on unlocking it because now I'm just feeling irritated.

"You know," I say, "this was a mistake. Go get back in your fancy-ass car and leave, okay?"

He crowds me against the wall, blocking me in with his arms. Arms which look muscular and powerful and oh, so commanding. He could pick me up, throw me over his shoulder, and haul me back to the car himself, probably while carrying my suitcase at the same time.

He opens his mouth to say something, but my apartment door swings open. Standing just inside is none other than Greg, my cheating ex and roommate.

"Samantha," Greg says, his icy blue eyes big with surprise as he takes in my position against the wall with Gideon. Greg cut his hair recently. The buzz cut of his pale, pale blond hair makes him look nearly bald.

"Greg," I say.

"Um." He looks from me to Gideon. "What are you doing out here?"

I groan. I can't do this. I can't verbally spar with both of these guys at once. At least with Gideon, it's usually kind of fun. I get to needle him until he breaks. But Greg? He's an asswipe. There's nothing fun about pissing him off.

"Nothing," I say, sounding as exhausted as I feel. "How about you?"

"I thought I heard your voice, and I wanted to talk to you right away." He looks at Gideon again, nervous.

"Would you just say it, then?" I snap.

"Look, don't be mad at me," he says, rubbing the shitty tattoo on his forearm like he always does when he's nervous. It's a guitar, and I swear he likes to imagine he's strumming it or something. "I left this afternoon. I came back, and your room was like this. I swear, I had nothing to do with it."

"My room was like *what*?" Fear pushes me to shove past him, Gideon on my heels.

We go through the living room, down the hall to the master bedroom. I stop on the threshold, because I feel like I've been punched in the gut.

The whole room is trashed.

Clothes are everywhere—the floor, the bed, flung over the lamp and the tiny desk I never work at. The dresser drawers are all pulled out, lying crooked on the floor. Someone searched my dresser, that much is obvious. What about the rest of the room? The desk looks untouched. My bed isn't made, but I never make it, and the blankets don't look any different than they did when I left this morning. My gaze flicks to my nightstand, where I keep my vibrator. The drawer is thankfully shut. But intact nightstand or not, my clothes have been messed with, and an icky feeling of violation creeps throughout my body.

"Sam?" Gideon whispers. "You okay?"

"Yeah, of course," I say brightly. "I'm fine."

"How long were you gone?" Gideon says.

I blink at him. "What?"

"No, you," he says, pointing at Greg. "How long were you out with the door unlocked?"

Greg gets a stubborn look on his face, like he isn't going to answer, but Gideon only stares harder at him.

"A couple of hours," Greg finally says.

"Karl must've been watching your apartment," Gideon says.

"What? Karl? You think Uncle Karl did this?" I sputter. "Why on earth would he break into my apartment and fling my clothes around?"

"Everything he does is about money, Samantha." Gideon's gaze is serious as he looks into my face. "Everything. You don't know him like I do."

"Dude, what exactly do you have against him?" I ask. "He's done nothing to me. Nothing."

Gideon pointedly looks around my room.

"This could've been anyone," I say. "It could've been Greg, or Addison."

Greg holds up his hands. "No way, I didn't do this—"

I continue, ignoring him. "Addison was pissed about someone eating her yogurt. Maybe she..."

But she wouldn't. Addison and I aren't friends anymore, but she wouldn't do something like this. And Greg, stupid ass that he is, genuinely seems upset about it, so I don't think he did it. He's just an idiot. I hate him, too—both him and Addison—but none of us are enemies.

"Gideon, whatever falling out you had with Karl is in the past," I say. "Honestly, he couldn't have been hoping to find money in my clothes."

"Or money at all," Greg says with a snicker. "You're poor as fuck, Samantha."

Gideon shoots me a puzzled glance, but I just shrug. I don't have to explain myself to him.

"Let's clean up and you can pack some things," Gideon says to me, steering me farther into the room.

It's physically difficult to make my feet take steps. I don't want to be in this room at all. And to think, a few minutes ago, I had been hoping to ignore Gideon's summons to Clear Springs. Not a chance of that, now. I *want* to go up there and get away from this mess, this violation.

Stupid Greg hovers in the doorway for a moment before clearing his throat and saying, "Uh, I'll be...I have to go to the store," and practically running away. Freaking coward.

Gideon snorts in disgust, then says, "Okay, where's your suitcase?"

I look around the room. "I'm not wearing any of these clothes without washing them first."

"That's fine," he says. "There's a washer and dryer at home."

"At your place."

He spots my suitcase, which is still resting in front of the closet where I left it after getting back from Hawaii. "It's *our* place, Sam. It always has been."

"Not by choice," I mutter.

He takes a step back, as if I've hit him. Then he seems to collect himself and he opens up the suitcase with quick, jerky movements. As I start picking out the clothes I want to bring with me to Clear Springs, he tidies up whatever I leave in my wake. I want to shout at him to quit being helpful, but that would take too much energy.

Today has been a roller-coaster, and I just want to get out of this apartment and feel safe again.

Gideon

Samantha gets on her phone as soon as we're back in my car. She speaks calmly and carefully to the person on the other end of the line, apologizing and explaining that she needs to take a few days off from work because of a family emergency.

"Thanks, Izzie," she says. "I'm sorry to leave you in a bind." She gives a little chuckle. "True enough. All right. I'm sorry—okay, I'll stop saying 'sorry.' See you soon, I hope."

Ending the call, she slips the phone back into her bag and looks out the window at the passing city. We're about to get on the freeway heading north.

"Is everything going to be okay with you taking more time off?" I ask.

"Yep."

"You know, you don't really need to have a job at all. Your allowance should be plenty, even when living in San Esteban."

"Yep." She scowls and looks away.

"Is there some reason you're not using your allowance?" I ask.

Her glare shouldn't be sexy, but it kinda is. Especially after watching her spread her pussy lips right here in this car and get herself off. Her glare is sexy, her smile is sexy, her everything is sexy. She opened up the Pandora's box of her sexiness, and now it's impossible to put those images away again.

"I'm not using my allowance because it comes from *you*," she snaps. "And I don't need it anyway, so leave me alone."

Was I thrilled about suddenly having an eight-year-old girl come to live with me? Of course not. But that had nothing to do with Samantha, and everything to do with my best friend and his wife dying suddenly. There was also the fact that I'd been twenty-five years old at the time, with absolutely no fucking idea of how to take care of a child. I was grieving and confused.

Since she left for college, I tried to help her out by giving her an allowance from my own funds, because her trust isn't available to her yet.

Apparently, she's pretending the allowance doesn't exist.

I understand why she hates me. I was a shitty guardian to her. I withdrew emotionally, right when she needed it.

But every time she lashes out? It makes me want to pull her closer and make up for all the wrong I did.

TWELVE

Gideon

It's about a two-hour drive between San Esteban and Clear Springs, although rush-hour traffic from evening commuters slows us down. Samantha falls asleep, her head lolling to the side and knocking into the window occasionally. She looks massively uncomfortable, so I scoot over to the center seat and angle her body towards mine so she can use my shoulder as a pillow. It's not a soft shoulder, but it has to be better than glass.

Why is it now, several years after she grew up in my home, that I can finally offer the support I should've been giving her all along?

I've grown up—that must be part of it. But there's more to it than this.

I don't know what the fuck happened with her apartment, but now that Karl's sniffing around her again, plus whatever that was, whether it was Karl or not, she needs protection. She doesn't want me there, that much is obvious. Hiring someone is the best option.

Lucky for me, I have friends in the security sector. I text Ryder Callihan.

Hey, sorry to bug you but I have a job for Ironwood that I want to run past you.

Yeah, I'm texting him even though he and Jaxon are still on their honeymoon with Olivia. I figure if Ryder doesn't want to respond, he won't, whereas Jaxon would feel more responsibility and respond even if he doesn't feel like it.

Luck is still on my side, because Ryder texts back immediately. *What's up? Who needs protecting?*

My... What do I call Samantha? My ward? I delete the "my" and write, *A woman I take care of.*

Does he know about Samantha's and my connection? I'm about to add it to my response, but he writes back first.

Where does she live? What kind of work does she do?

Sighing, I write, *You know her. It's Samantha, Olivia's friend.*

Holy shit, no way.

I don't have a response for that, so I just wait.

Sure enough, he writes again, *Okay, we can protect her. I'll send someone over to do a threat assessment and interview.*

We're on our way to Clear Springs right now, I write.

No problem, our guys travel.

Thanks man.

A minute passes, then two. My phone screen goes black for a moment before lighting up again.

One of our guys will be there at ten tomorrow morning. And you're welcome, happy to help you and Samantha out.

I exhale deeply and look down at Samantha. Her eyes are closed, and her long lashes captivate me. So do her freckles. I've never been this close to her, never allowed more than cursory hugs when she was small, and then we didn't exchange any physical affection when she got older. I left all of that to Carolina, Samantha's nanny.

The scenery changes from flat freeway to winding hills, and then we're home. Clay steers the car along the driveway and into the garage.

Samantha wakes up at the sound of the garage door lowering behind us. "We're here?"

"Yep."

I get her bags and lead her from the car and into the house, then down the hall to her bedroom. She follows along, clutching my hand. My heart pangs with regret and an overwhelming need. I don't understand this—it doesn't make sense. None of it makes sense, and none of it has made sense since Matt and Cassie died and left me with their little girl.

Her room hasn't changed from when she moved to San Esteban for college. I haven't touched a single thing in here. It's been cleaned regularly, just like the rest of the house, but that's it.

I guess a part of me kept hoping she'd come home.

Samantha, eyes half open, kicks off her shoes and crawls into her bed fully clothed.

I pull the comforter up to her chin and whisper, "Goodnight."

Samantha

As Gideon leaves the room, I snuggle down into my bed, eased by its familiarity. Yet I just had a long nap in the car, and now I'm nowhere near tired. I scramble from the bed and see my purse on the floor next to the nightstand. Fishing my phone out of it, I see that it's only nine p.m.

Yeah, I definitely can't sleep now.

The house's air conditioner kicks on, throwing a chill into the room.

My messenger bag is next to my suitcase. I tug my laptop from it and power on the machine while I carry it over to my desk.

The desk's surface is littered in jars stuffed with pens and highlighters, a stack of sticker sheets, and along the back, a row of books about the craft of writing. I run a finger over their worn spines. I have everything from the technical how-tos, like *Scene and Sequel* by Jack Bickham and *Story* by Robert McKee, to the inspirational, like *Bird by Bird* by Anne Lamott and *On Writing* by Stephen King. Classics, all of them. I've learned so much.

I wonder if any of these authors suspected I'd be using their teachings to write smut. I hope they'd be amused by it.

I flip on the desk lamp. My laptop's ready, the word processing program open and ready to go. Where were we before? Oh, right, Alex the bodyguard and Calliope were admitting to feelings. I read the last few paragraphs I'd written, then start adding, my fingers tapping quickly, the words coming out without thought. This scene I'm writing, it's coming from somewhere deep inside me, somewhere beneath my own thoughts.

HE DROPPED HIS HEAD. "Which is why this won't work. I can't do my job if there are feelings in the way."

"That doesn't make any sense—"

"It's how it has to be." He turned to walk away.

She reached out and grabbed his arm. "Don't go. I want you. I...I need you. All my life, I've wanted you. Maybe I have daddy issues, maybe it's stupid. But I can't let you go. I don't care that you're so much older than I am. It doesn't bother me."

"Well, it bothers me, Calliope. It's wrong. I don't want to prey on you, and that's what this would be."

IS *that* why Gideon seemed so reluctant in the car? He talked about going to hell. He said, "Make it good. If I'm going to hell, I may as well enjoy it."

I thought I'd made it good. Even now, I close my eyes and remember the way he'd watched me while I'd gotten off. His eyes—it was like he physically could not look away.

Shifting in my desk chair, I subtly try to relieve the empty, aching pressure between my legs. Wiggling around is not good enough. I need touch, contact on my sensitive clit.

I peer over my shoulder to the cracked bedroom door behind me. The hallway is dark. The house is silent. It's only nine, but maybe Gideon's as tired as I was, and he didn't have a nap in the car. He's probably in bed for the night, or at least he retreated to his office. I swear, he's married to that cold, ugly office.

So I'm safe here. I scoot forward in my chair, slouching enough to spread my legs and sneak one hand under my skirt to my panties. They're already damp, so I shove them aside and stroke directly against my folds.

It feels so. Damn. Good. Especially when I close my eyes and think about Gideon watching me. Only in this fantasy, he's grabbing my hand and flinging it aside.

"Mine," he said, anchoring her hand in place. "I'll take care of this pretty little cunt. Let Daddy do it."

No, not *Daddy*, I think. *Sir*, or *Master*. *Daddy*'s just…too much.

And then he would bring his own hand to my pussy, and part my folds so he can examine me, scrutinize every little bit. He'd lean forward and lick over me, tasting me.

A soft whimper escapes my throat, but I swallow the other sounds that want release. My hips buck forward against my hand, the hand I'm imagine is his hand, his lips, his tongue.

"Once wasn't enough today?"

The low, warm voice startles me and I freeze.

Keeping perfectly still, because moving my arm now would give me away even more than my spread-legged position, I say, "I don't know what you're talking about."

"I want to come into your bedroom," he says, his voice quiet and even. "I want to watch you come again. But I'm only doing that if you tell me I can. You have to want it, too."

I don't know what to say. Do I want him to come in here? Do I want to see where this dark, twisted thing between us can go? Yes, yes I do.

"If you don't say anything, I'll turn around now," he says. "We never have to talk about it again. I'll pretend you were just sitting in your desk chair, very energetically *typing*."

"Stay," I whisper.

"Sorry, I didn't catch that."

I'm pretty sure he heard me, the infuriating man.

"Come in," I say. "Watch me again."

I look at my laptop, and I can see his reflection in the screen. He's getting closer and closer. Then he's right behind me, resting his hands on the back of my desk chair. He's close enough I can smell the faint lemon scent of his hand soap, and the woodsmoke that clings to him constantly. He's close enough that he'll be able to see the words on the screen in front of me. If he reads them, he'll know.

"Well, it bothers me," Gideon reads. *"It's wrong. I don't want to prey on you, and that's what this would be.* As in literature, so also in life, is that what you're doing, Sam?"

I shrug, and the movement causes my shoulders to brush up against his hands. Slowly, so slowly, he spins me around in my desk chair. I'm facing him now, my face level with his stomach. I flick my gaze down and see his jeans are very, very tight, straining over a bulge in the denim. My former guardian is very, very well-endowed.

"It *is* wrong," he says, palming himself over the front of his jeans. "Just like it says there, on your computer. Fuck. Do you think I'm preying on you?"

"No." I lift up my skirt, show him my panties. I'm

not sure if he can see the drenched center from his position, but my fingers glisten in the faint light coming from the desk lamp. "Maybe *I'm* preying on *you*."

He laughs and his brilliant eyes lift in amusement. Thankfully, his laugh isn't the sort that makes me feel foolish. His lips tug up on one side in a smirk. "You're preying on me? Then come and get me, precious girl."

There isn't really anywhere to go to get him—he's standing right here. But I understand what he's saying. He wants me to reach out and take what I want.

Well, right now? What I want is his dick. Specifically, I want it in my mouth and in my pussy and hell, I've never done it before but I'd probably take it in my ass, too, if he wanted to do that.

With shaking fingers, I unbutton his jeans. They're worn, and the buttons free easily. Then I'm staring at Gideon's boxers, with his cock pushing out against the fabric. He's solid, girthy. His cock has a commanding, irrepressible presence to it, just like the man. I push his jeans and boxers down and wrap my hand around his cock.

Heavy, warm. The skin stretched tight over the rock-hard organ. The tip tempts me. I want to lick it, suck it, put it in my mouth.

"You keep looking at me like that," Gideon says, "and I don't know what I'm going to do."

I lean forward in my chair and press a kiss to the tip of his cock. Gideon groans and cups the side of my head. He's not pushing me farther down on his cock or doing anything to control my movements—it's more like he's touching me to see if I'm real. Or maybe I'm projecting, because this moment is just like that moment in the back of his car. Is this really, truly happening? Or am I in some kind of wonderful dream?

If it's a dream, I don't want to wake up.

But if it's real, what now?

"I finally have you," I gasp, "and I don't know what to do. Why don't I know what to do?"

"I can take charge," he says, looking down at me with what I can only describe as fondness.

"Maybe?" I squeak.

"Do you want me to bend you over the desk like Maxwell does to Tabitha in *My Hot Professor*?" he asks.

My Hot Professor. I wrote that book. Or rather, "Sammie Starr" wrote that book. Wait a minute. Gideon knows the character names. He knows the desk scene.

"You...you've read *My Hot Professor*?" I ask.

He laughs, a low, lazy sound. "Oh, precious girl. I've read every single one of your books."

THIRTEEN

Gideon

"And...and you know they're *my* books?" she asks.

The uncertain look on her face just undoes me. I want to wipe it away, see it replaced with the reckless confidence she'd shown me in the car.

"Of course I knew they were your books, S*ammie*," I say, cupping her cheek. "I'm probably your number one fan."

My dick is jutting forward, held lightly in her hand, level with her mouth. She stares up at me in surprise.

"How long have you known?" she asks.

"Since the first book you sent. You didn't honestly think I wouldn't know, did you?"

"Well, you never said anything, and I didn't even think you were downloading the books."

"The first cover was a picture of a woman with her hands down her panties. Of course I downloaded the book."

She gives a little laugh and glances away.

I steer her face back so we're looking at each other. "We don't have to do any of this, Sam."

"Stop trying to talk me out of it," she says, sticking out her stubborn little chin. "I want you. Don't you want me?"

She speaks in the voice of a woman, but underneath the words is the thread of insecurity, the insecurity of a little girl. Fuck. I shouldn't be doing this.

But then she takes me in her mouth, all the way, sucking me down, and all reason leaves my mind. Her warm, hot tongue slides along my shaft.

All right. Yeah. We're doing this.

Reluctantly, I pull out of the paradise of her mouth. I'm in this for more than a blowjob. Like I said in the car earlier today, if I'm going to hell, I want to enjoy it. And I want to do it all.

Samantha blinks up at me, her lips slightly parted.

"Sit on the bed," I say.

She doesn't question me, just gets up and walks over to do as I said. My dick was already hard but her obedience makes me harder. She doesn't know this about me, yet. Or maybe she's guessed? The number of heavy-handed heroes in her books, always quick to spank, and then quick to praise, makes me think Samantha knows me better than I ever intended.

I reach under her skirt and find the sides of her panties. I yank them down and drop the garment on the floor next to us.

"Samantha," I say.

"Don't you dare tell me we can still quit," she warns.

"You don't make the calls here, sweetheart," I say. "That's up to me. And I need you to know you're safe. If you don't like something, tell me and we stop to figure it out, or we stop entirely."

"Got it," she says, biting her lip and eyeing my cock.

"Good." I flip up her skirt, revealing her pussy to me for the second time today, this time without those panties in the way. She has a faint thatch of dark blond curls, well-trimmed at the top, and then pretty pink lips, glossy with her arousal.

Slowly, so slowly, I drag the head of my cock over her folds, playing in her wetness. She writhes, lifts her hips, trying to get an angle, trying to tempt me inside of her slick, wet heat. But we're missing an important step. I'm so blinded by lust and my own eagerness to be inside of her, I almost forgot.

"Condom," I say, pulling back. "I have a box in my bathroom."

She tightens her fists on the sheets, gasps, "My bag. It's closer."

I reach down and grab her bag, hand it to her. She

rifles through it and pulls out a foil wrapper before thrusting it at me.

"Eager girl." I put on the condom, then flip her over to her stomach and cover her with my body. She moans and arches her back, with her ass rubbing against my cock. I shove up her skirt, loving that we're both half-dressed, loving that we didn't take the time to get completely naked.

"Tell me what he did to you," I whisper in her ear.

Samantha's voice is muffled against the mattress. "He—what? Who?"

"The guy in the hotel," I say. "Terrence. Tell me again what you told me in the car. Tell me everything that I was listening to that night."

Her smile is devilish as she looks over her shoulder at me. "He told me to run, and he chased me around to the other side of the bed."

"Really," I say in interest. So Terrence might have a primal kink.

"He caught me really quickly. When I tried to get away, he spanked me."

"I heard that spank," I say, relishing the memory.

She moans. "He put me on all fours. Then he kneeled behind me and ate me out."

I picture it, Samantha's body open for his mouth. I imagine myself sitting in one of those hotel chairs on the balcony, looking in at them, watching him spank her, then pin her down on all fours so he could taste her.

"After that, he bent me over the dresser so we could see each other in the mirror. Then he fucked me—hard. He had to put his hand over my mouth because I was too loud—I was disturbing the neighbor."

I can't hold back any longer. I press into her waiting pussy. It's a tight fit, but she's so slippery, I'm confident that her moans are of pleasure and not pain.

"Doing all right?" I ask, my voice gruff.

"Yeah. Better than all right," she says, giving a little wriggle.

I lean back and smack her ass. Not too hard, just enough to let her know I can. She moans again and her pussy flutters around me.

"Did you like it when he spanked you?" I ask.

"It hurt," she says.

"But did you like it?"

She nods into the sheets but doesn't speak out loud.

I spank her again. "Answer me, little girl."

Her pussy clenches hard around my cock. Yes, she liked it. She liked it then and she likes it now. I just want to hear her say it.

"Samantha," I say in warning.

"Yes," she gasps. "Yes, I liked it."

"Good," I murmur, stroking my palms over the light pink marks on her ass cheek. I press the rest of the way inside of her until I'm in as far as I can go. She flexes around me, squeezing gently. "Just breathe, precious girl. You're doing so good. So good for me."

Leaning over her, covering her body with mine, I

begin to stroke within her. A distant part of my mind is shouting that this isn't right, that I shouldn't be touching her or even thinking about her like this. But I shove that part aside in favor of making Samantha feel good, of making myself feel good, of claiming this woman.

"You're mine," I whisper, stroking harder and faster.

She lifts her hips, tries to thrust back. I use her movement to get a hand beneath her and find her clit.

"Gideon," she gasps. "Yes, right there."

She's so wet, my fingers slip easily over the little nub, back and forth while I fuck her.

"I'm going to come," she says, with the word *come* ending on a long moan.

"Come for me," I tell her. "Come for me, even though you were coming on that other cock less than a week ago. Come on *my* cock."

Her body goes rigid and she cries out, so loud it's almost a scream, just like she did in that hotel room with Terrence. I bite her neck because I can't help myself, but I try not to break skin.

"Yes, yes, yes," she chants. "Harder."

I don't know if she means the pounding I'm giving her or the way I've clamped my teeth over her flesh, but I intensify both.

She screams again, and her pussy clamps down on me, rhythmically squeezing. I lift her up so I can grab her tits and put a foot on the edge of the bed to change my angle slightly.

"Was it like this?" I pant. "Did he hold you like this?"

"A little." She moves my hands to a slightly different angle, then pulls one down to band around her stomach. "When he came, he held me like this."

I'm not going to be able to hold off my orgasm much longer. I both want it and dread it. I want to do this all night with her.

"You wish you were there," she says in wonder, her hand on my forearm that goes around her torso. "You wish you were watching."

I nod, but I'm not sure if she can see it while I finish thrusting. My orgasm is fierce, tearing through my body like a drug, tensing my muscles and expelling pleasure.

"Gideon?" she asks.

"Yeah, yeah, that's what I wish." I admit, breathing heavily.

"You like to watch," she says, her chest heaving as I fall to the bed and tug her against my side.

"Yeah, I like to watch."

"And you like to spank."

"I didn't hurt you, did I?"

"Not at all."

"Then yeah," I say. "I like to spank. And sometimes I might want to make it hurt, if you consent."

"We could talk about that," she says. "I'm not necessarily against it."

This is all assuming we'll do this again. I want to. I need to just turn my brain off and forget the complicated history I have with her. Because without that history, nothing would be holding me back from calling her mine.

My precious girl.

Samantha

We fuck again in the middle of the night. A little more spanking. A little more talk about my night with Terrence. It really seems to get Gideon off, the recollection of what I did with another man. I don't understand it, but I love how it makes him lose control. I learn more about him in the course of twenty-four hours than I've learned in the years I lived here. The thought is sobering and exciting at the same time.

And then in the morning, we fuck again. Apparently, now that we've finally let down this wall between us, we can't keep our hands off of each other.

Gideon fixes me breakfast from some prepared meals left by his housekeeper.

"You look cute in my t-shirt," he says while he plates the food.

I can only grin at him. I'm wearing it less because

of the cuteness factor and more because it smells like him. When he's not looking, I pull the collar up to my nose and inhale. Woodsmoke. Gideon's scent.

I get out my laptop to write while I eat, and he doesn't seem to mind, just kisses my forehead and says, "I'm going to take a quick shower. Don't eat all the cantaloupe."

I stare at his retreating back. How does he know that cantaloupe is my favorite thing? He was never around for breakfasts with me when I was a kid.

Whatever. This book isn't going to write itself.

"IF YOU WANT to do this, you need to know a few things about me," Alex said.

Calliope stared up at him, her heart pounding. "What do I need to know?"

He tugged her into his lap. "I'm damaged inside. There are dark, dark thoughts in my head. Thoughts of pain mixed with pleasure. And when we're done, I'm going to leave. Because I have these feelings, I will leave."

Tears pricked her eyes. "I don't understand. Feelings should make you stay."

"I'm twisted inside. And I will leave. And you might feel hurt by this, but it'll be nothing on how I feel. Wrecked."

. . .

OOH, that's a new title idea. I could make this less trope-y of a title and simply call it *Wrecked*. But *Wrecked* has probably been used as a romance title a thousand times, so I make a note in the manuscript to do a search on book retailers. Copyright doesn't cover titles in the US, but I'd rather not use a title everyone else has already used.

The doorbell rings before I can get back into the scene. My head shoots up. Who would be here at...I check the time. Nine-thirty?

The sound of Gideon's shower is faint from upstairs. I hurry up and knock on his bathroom door.

"Hey, someone's here. Are you expecting someone?"

"Yeah," Gideon calls over the sound of the running shower. "They're early. Go ahead and let them in. I'll be right out, ten minutes tops."

I'd rather not answer the door with wet hair while wearing one of Gideon's t-shirts and panties, nothing else. But the doorbell rings again, so I find a pair of jean shorts at the top of my suitcase and slide them on before rushing back downstairs.

It's only when I reach the entryway that I realize I should've put on a bra. Well, too late for that, I guess. Taking a deep breath, I unlock the door and pull it open.

Then I slam the door shut again.

Because standing there on Gideon's front porch is none other than Terrence.

FOURTEEN

Samantha

I forget how to breathe.

Yep, the guy on the front porch is the same guy I just described in very fine detail last night to Gideon, recounting every position and every word between us. I told Gideon how Terrence chased me. How he fucked me. I showed Gideon exactly how Terrence held me when he came. It was sick, filthy.

And so fucking good.

Maybe I imagined seeing him? Like my brain has conjured this hallucination after talking about him so much yesterday. That would be understandable. It would make sense.

The doorbell rings again.

It's probably someone else, someone with Terrence's build and light brown skin.

"Samantha?" the man says from the other side.

Terrence's voice. And the guy knows my name.

So it's really Terrence. I didn't imagine him. Dammit. My heart trips triple-time in my chest. Panic-panic-panic.

He says, "Are you going to let me in?"

I don't think I will. Even though he can't see me, I shake my head. I'll just go upstairs and hide under my bed like a little kid. Because this is too weird.

Gideon said he was expecting someone. Was he expecting *Terrence*? Because that's just wrong. He wouldn't have set this up, would he? Like he arranged some sort of threesome while I was sleeping last night? I think he'd tell me, though.

"Samantha, are you safe?" Terrence asks.

That surprises me into opening the door again. Facing him once more, I say, "Yeah, I'm safe. Why?"

"Ironwood had a call. Gideon's hiring someone to protect you. So what happened?"

A little ember of anger stirs within me. Gideon's hiring protection? Without even asking me first?

"Did he specifically request *you*," I ask, "or is this just an unhappy coincidence?"

Terrence's eyebrows rise on his smooth forehead. "Unhappy?"

I fold my arms around myself, in part because I'm feeling stubborn as fuck, and in part to hide the fact I'm not wearing a bra.

"I don't know, it's just kind of odd that you're here."

"He didn't specifically request me, no. I was available, so Ironwood sent me up."

Well, that's a relief. I guess. I wonder how Gideon will react to Terrence's arrival. The shower is still running.

Terrence leans toward me, a curious expression on his face. He takes in my jean shorts, the oversized t-shirt, and my hair, which is probably crazy-looking right now. "You smell like sex."

He looks...amused. Dammit. Why does he think this is funny? I'm standing here in a t-shirt that's clinging to my shoulders for dear life, and I'm not wearing a bra.

Of course he thinks it's funny. Gideon said I look cute. But Terrence probably thinks I look ridiculous.

"I'm pretty sure you aren't here to talk about my sex life," I say. "You made it pretty clear you weren't a part of it after that night in Hawaii."

Ignoring that entirely, he peers past me into the house. "Are you going to invite me in?"

I step back from the door. "Sure, come on in."

Mentally, I high-five myself for not sounding sullen or suspicious—two things I am definitely feeling right now.

"So this is where you live, huh?" he asks. "Nice digs."

"I don't live here," I say. "Gideon does."

"And you're here because..."

Sighing, I say, "I grew up here."

"With Gideon."

"Yes, with Gideon. He was my guardian when I was growing up."

"Is he who you had sex with? Wow, that's twisted," he says.

"Says the guy who wanted to chase me and catch me and hold me down during sex," I shoot back.

"Fair enough. I didn't say there was anything wrong with it, though. Consenting adults and all that."

To anyone else, it will sound wrong, so wrong. Is that why Gideon held back, the past few years? Obviously he wouldn't touch me when I was a minor. But after that, when I sent him those books, when he knew I'd written them—why not then? It must've been how taboo the whole thing sounds when it's spelled out with the facts. The age gap, the former guardian and ward. But who cares what anyone else thinks, if we love each other? I'm not saying we do, yet, but we might. And if we loved each other, that would make everyone else's opinions nothing more than bullshit.

Terrence's opinion, included. Who cares what he thinks? I certainly don't.

"You can come into the kitchen. I'm having breakfast," I say, leading the way.

His eyes get big as he surveys the place. I guess the house is pretty big and fancy-looking. To me, it's just another house.

"Have you eaten?" I ask him. "I can fix you a plate."

"Nah, I'm good, thanks."

We move toward the table, but we don't sit down. I slam my laptop shut, just in case for some reason Terrence needs to walk past it. I don't want him to see what I'm writing.

His lips twitch. "Were you watching something you shouldn't be?"

I'm tempted to mess with him. In fact, the temptation is too strong to resist. So I lie: "Well, watching porn where hot guys chase down a girl and fuck her until she comes isn't against the law, is it?"

"You're watching porn with chasing? Do you need to be chased?"

Do I need to be chased? Yes, yes, yes, I think. *If you're doing the chasing.*

But I don't say it. I can't.

For a long moment, we stare at each other. Gideon's shower is still running in what seems to be the longest shower ever, but he'll finish up soon, right?

Terrence

She doesn't fool me for a second, the little liar. She wasn't watching porn and eating cantaloupe. Or if she was watching porn, she wasn't watching primal porn.

Damn, it would be hot if she was, though.

"Look," I say, "let's back up. I'm just here to interview you and Gideon for the job."

I'm trying to ignore the slope of her shoulder and the way the too-big t-shirt she's wearing drapes off, revealing what looks very much like a passionate bite mark from a set of human teeth. Right where her shoulder meets her neck.

Clearing my throat and forcing my gaze away from her shoulder to the spacious kitchen, I say, "After the interview, Ironwood will come up with a plan of protection."

"Should there be capitals on those p's?" Samantha interrupts. "Plan of Protection, with capital p's? I'm guessing Ironwood probably abbreviates it to POP?"

"Actually, yes," I say.

"And this is standard procedure for the company?"

"Yeah."

"How about for other security companies? Is it the same?"

"I'm not sure about that," I say slowly. "I've only worked at one other company, and we didn't use POPs; we called them Protection Schematics, or P Schemes. Do you want to get a notebook and pen, write this down?"

She looks for a moment as if she's considering it. Then she shakes her head. "Nah. I can remember."

She's a cryptic little thing. That's fine. I don't have room for curiosity or finding out why she has all these questions; I have a job to do here. And I need to remember that job.

Am I jealous of her and this Gideon guy? Hell yes, I am. Do I wish it was me who'd been here with her last night, fucking her so hard I had to bite her shoulder? Fuck, yes.

I wonder if she screamed when she came. I wonder if he covered her mouth like I did. Dammit, I'm getting hard. This isn't the time. I need to think about other things immediately. Things like...tile. The floor is a nice tile, with a subdued starburst pattern. I follow the pattern with my gaze, until it snags on Samantha's bare toes.

Bare toes, and bare feet, going up to long, bare legs. Her denim cut-offs are short and sexy, half-hidden by the oversized t-shirt.

"That's his shirt, isn't it?" I ask.

"Don't tell me you're jealous." Her blue eyes flash.

I am. "Not in the least."

We're quiet for a moment. Finally, Samantha says, "Can I get you a glass of water or something?"

"Sure, thanks."

She gets a glass from the cabinet and goes to the water spout on the fridge. "Ice?"

"No thanks."

I can't help but stare at her as she pours the water. I told her that night in Hawaii was a one-time thing. And yet I want more of her. Of course I do.

My thoughts are whirling around in my head, so

fast, I can barely land on one before a new one rears up.

She brings me the water and I think I say thanks, but I'm mostly looking at her mouth. Are her lips swollen? Maybe a little. I wonder if she gave him head. I wish she'd given me head. I bet she's amazing at it.

She called me *sir*, that night in Hawaii. Did she call Gideon *sir*, too? Just how submissive is she, how far does that go?

Suddenly, a new, ugly thought enters my head, and I can't help but blurt it out. "Tell me you didn't cheat on him with me."

She gives me an incredulous look, her eyes widening. "Jeez, no. Of course not."

I don't know why I care. I *shouldn't* care. And yet I can't keep myself from asking, "So the two of you aren't exclusive?"

Don't touch her, I tell myself. She's a client, I tell myself. A very hot client whose body knows exactly how to respond to yours.

"No," she says quietly, "we're not exclusive."

"Good." I set down my glass of water. Leaning forward, I tilt Samantha's chin up and kiss her luscious lips.

She tastes sweet, like some kind of fruit. Probably cantaloupe, because there's some on the table next to us. I part her lips with mine and lick my tongue against hers, tasting more of her sweetness.

Last night, or maybe just a few minutes ago, was he

kissing her in this exact same way? Did he put as much thought and care into it as I am now? Because this girl is delicious, and the tiny sound she makes in the back of her throat is so sweet, so arousing, it makes me think I could do this forever.

Could he?

At first, she doesn't do more than move her lips with mine. But when I keep going, when I don't end the kiss, she grabs my arms and clings to me, her body flush against mine. Our tongues twine together, slipping and sliding as our bodies did that night. She moans softly and that little sound brings even more of the night back. I loved watching us in the mirror, her tits moving with each of my forceful strokes. I loved watching the way her lips parted, and then, after I covered her mouth, the fiery blaze of lust in her eyes, followed by the way her eyes closed and her face twisted in pleasure.

I grab her denim-clad ass, tugging her closer. Nothing matters more in this moment than tasting this beautiful girl, showing her with my lips and tongue how much I've missed her since our night together. Nothing matters more than taking every breath, every sound she makes and filing it away to remember later, when no doubt she'll still be here with Gideon and I'll be alone in my comfortable little duplex.

She rubs her chest against mine. I can feel the points of her hardened nipples. I want to flip up her shirt and bite her, give her some real friction and feeling to get her going.

If I flip up her shirt, those gorgeous breasts will be there, ready for my lips and teeth, my pinching fingers. Samantha won't be able to stand it—she'll cry out and—

A deep voice penetrates the moment. "Should I come back later, or do you want me to watch?"

Samantha gasps and pushes away from me. Or maybe she's trying to push me away from her, but I don't budge. I do let her go, though.

We turn together and face Gideon, who's standing in the kitchen doorway, running a towel over his wet hair.

FIFTEEN

Gideon

So, okay. Just a couple of hours ago, I was screwing Samantha's brains out like the dirty old pervert I am. And now I find her plastered to the bodyguard she fucked in Hawaii.

It's...unexpected.

Rage-inducing.

Hot.

Samantha's cheeks are bright pink and she clears her throat once, then again.

"Um, Gideon," she says, "you remember Terrence Johnson, from the wedding, right?"

"Yes," I say, tossing my towel on the counter and striding forward to shake his hand. "Although I don't think I'm quite as well-acquainted with him as you are, Sam."

She coughs and hisses, "*Gideon.*"

Terrence smiles. "No, that's deserved. I apologize, Mr. Woodhouse—that was completely unprofessional of me. I assure you, it won't happen again. This isn't how Ironwood operates."

"I appreciate that," I say. "No harm done. Please, call me Gideon."

"Gideon," he says, nodding. "Call me Terrence."

Good, so he and I are back to where we were when we met in Hawaii. First-name basis. Could be friends, even. He seemed easy enough to talk to, although our chat was very brief then, and it'll be all business, now.

At my nod, he takes out his phone and says, "I'll be taking notes on my phone, if that's all right?" When neither of us protests, he goes on, "Okay, so I'm here because Samantha needs a personal security detail. Would you two talk to me a little about the threat?"

"There haven't been any threats," Samantha says.

"Her uncle is back in California," I say, "and I don't trust him."

"He's not a bad guy," Samantha insists. "You just don't like him because he wanted to take care of me when I was a kid."

"I don't like him because he wanted to take your money," I say.

Terrence looks between the two of us, waiting to see if Samantha will argue back. Rolling her eyes, she says, "Obviously we disagree about this threat. But my room at my apartment was messed up yesterday, and I think that's the larger concern, but hardly worthy of full-time bodyguards."

"Why don't we let the guy in the business tell us whether or not it's worthy," I say lightly. I don't know if I want to fight with her or fuck her. Both, I guess. She's being so stubborn. Could I kiss her into submission?

Could *we* kiss her into submission, Terrence and I?

The salacious thought is a turn-on, but in the end, I don't want to share her. I just finally got her into bed, I've finally given in to the lustful urges I've had since she slid that first erotic story under my door, right before she left for college. I'm not ready to share her, and I've never done that before, anyway. I don't know that I could share any woman, much less Samantha.

"What's the story with your apartment?" Terrence asks her.

Is it just me, or does he look concerned for her? Perhaps more concerned than an impartial bodyguard would normally be?

"My dresser was emptied," she says. "That's all that I noticed."

"Do you have roommates?" he asks.

"Two. A man and a woman. He's my ex, and she's a former friend."

"An ex and a former friend. So, a hostile living environment," Terrence says.

"We're civil, actually," Samantha says. "It's not comfortable, but I think I hate them more than they hate me. And my hatred isn't even strong enough to throw out Addison's yogurt, tempting as that is."

"The guy seemed to feel pretty bad about Samantha's room," I add.

Terrence nods. "Were any of your clothes missing?"

"I don't think so?" Samantha says. "I didn't exactly take inventory or anything. I just grabbed what I wanted and brought it here. I still want to use the washing machine," she says to me.

"As soon as we're done here," I promise.

"Other than the apartment break-in, has anything else threatening happened?" Terrence asks. "Any other attacks?"

"Can we really call that an attack?" Samantha asks.

"Anything that harms or threatens your person or your personal belongings is categorized as an attack," Terrence says. "Ironwood takes those things seriously. Offenders often escalate when they don't get the reaction they want, or when they don't accomplish their goal. If this was done by your roommates, and the goal is to get you to leave, then they have accomplished it."

"Not for long," Samantha says. "I'm going back."

"What?" I say sharply.

"It's not like I can stay here," she says with a rueful smile. "I mean, I have a life down there in San Esteban. A job. Friends."

I don't know why I had pictured her coming back to live here for good, but I did. I never thought her library work was something she was passionate about, but maybe I was wrong.

All I know is that in my head, Samantha is done with San Esteban. In my head, she's living here at the house again, only we don't sleep in separate rooms, and we fuck all the time, unable to keep our hands off of each other.

And she's shutting that fantasy down, right here, right now while this other man is in the room—another man who has touched her and kissed her like I want to be doing right now.

There's *my* bite mark on her shoulder. Did he see that? He must have. And he kissed her anyway.

I feel like I'm going to explode.

"I'll be back in a minute," I say tightly. "Try to keep your clothes on."

Leaving the room, I try to get my breathing under control. I stand in the foyer for a long moment, listening to the rise and fall of their voices. Terrence is asking Samantha questions about her life in San Esteban—her routine, the building where she works, who she spends her free time with, and where she does it.

I realize I'm curious about her answers. I want to know more about her life, what she does.

A couple more deep breaths, and I go back into the kitchen.

"Oh, good," Terrence says when he sees me. "I

want to talk over a few more things for you, what your ideal set-up is—"

"Um, isn't *my* ideal set-up what we need to be considering?" Samantha asks.

"Of course," he says. "We already discussed yours. As Gideon is the one who called Ironwood, I want to get a fuller picture from him. It's all part of the routine."

I pour some coffee and the three of us sit down at the kitchen table, going over details of what kind of protection I think Samantha should have (lots) and how much she's willing to tolerate (a little).

Terrence types away in his phone, taking notes. After a few more minutes of discussing every possible scenario, he says, "I'd like to bring in Ryder or Jaxon on this, so we can do a final check. But for now, what I'm thinking is light, twenty-four-hour security—"

"What?" Samantha interrupts.

"But at a distance," Terrence finishes.

I frown. I'd rather her bodyguards be on her at all times.

"And by 'light' security," he clarifies, "I mean one guard at a time."

"One?" I say. "What if they have to take a break, or take a piss, or whatever?"

"Breaks will only be taken when the client is secure," Terrence says. "Or we could do shorter, four- or six-hour shifts, eliminate the need for breaks—"

"Yes, let's do that," I say.

"You'll be paying a lot extra for that," Terrence says.

I nod. "It's worth it."

Raising a hand, Samantha says, "And do I get any decision-making power in this?"

"Of course," Terrence says.

"It sure doesn't seem that way," she says.

I can tell I've pushed her too far with all of this. "Look, you can make lots of choices, decisions, whatever. Just not about cutting back on security."

"Anything else, though?" she asks.

I stare into her eyes. "Yes, anything else."

"Excellent." She turns in her chair to look at Terrence. "I want to go back to San Esteban. Immediately. Terrence, can you give me a ride?"

"Wait a second," I say, "that's not what I meant—"

"I'm an adult, Gideon," she says in a cutting voice, with a glare just as cutting. "You're not my daddy, you don't get to boss me around or spank me when I misbehave."

I only get to spank you when I'm fucking you, I think, but I don't say it out loud.

Samantha

Gideon carries my suitcase out of his house.

I'm pissed at him, and I was hoping for a reaction,

and I'm already regretting my proclamation that I'm going to leave. Why doesn't he ask me to stay? Shouldn't he ask me? I want him to ask me, or at least, I think I do.

He and I need to talk. We had sex—so much sex—and we didn't get to talk about what it might mean, do we want to do this again, were we just "getting it out of our systems," or what.

My heart aches as Terrence opens the trunk of his SUV and Gideon slides my suitcase into it. Maybe I should stay here, work things out with Gideon.

But if I stay, we're just going to get back in bed and I seriously doubt any talking will happen. He'll still be as bossy as ever, trying to dictate my life in San Esteban. I still won't know what kind of relationship we have. So as much as it hurts, distance is what we need right now.

At least, that's what I tell myself as Terrence pulls out of the driveway and my heart shatters into approximately three million fifty-eight pieces.

It shouldn't hurt to breathe. All I can think about is running off to college like I did when I was eighteen. Here I am five years later, leaving behind the man I love again, and believing he will never love me in the same way.

"Are you doing all right?" Terrence asks.

"Yeah," I say, fighting to keep my voice steady. "I'm fine."

He doesn't speak again until we're on the freeway.

"I just need to be sure. He doesn't seem like the kind of guy who would coerce someone, but did he—"

"No," I say, and my voice has more strength in it. "He didn't coerce me. Everything was consensual."

"Okay." He doesn't take his eyes off the road. "Good."

I'm not sure what to say to that, so I say nothing. The drive goes on in relative quiet. I think of suggesting music, then just as quickly shoot down my own idea before voicing it.

We're not far from San Esteban when Terrence speaks again. "Hunter, from Ironwood, is going to be at your apartment when I bring you home."

"Not you?"

"No, I'm not working today, other than this consult Ryder asked me to do as a favor."

"But you're already here—"

His hands tighten on the steering wheel and his voice is harsh when he says, "I said I can't."

"Right."

I had to say goodbye to Gideon because I was stubborn, and now I'll have to say goodbye to Terrence, and why does this day feel so completely shitty? I woke up feeling sated and happy, but everything's different now.

"Sorry, I shouldn't snap," Terrence says. "I'm in a bad mood."

He doesn't seem angry, really. I take a good look at him. No, he's not angry. He's sad.

"Terrence," I say quietly, putting my hand on his forearm, "what happened?"

"It's nothing." He shakes his head and rolls his shoulders, dislodging my hand from his arm. "I just learned another buddy of mine died on the job."

"Someone from Ironwood?" I ask, my heart picking up in fear.

He shakes his head. "No. I worked with him before coming to Cali. But he was a good guy, and I just found out yesterday, and I didn't sleep great last night. I shouldn't take it out on you."

"I'm sorry he died," I say. "That must be especially hard, after…"

I trail off. I'm afraid to say his name. I barely knew the guy.

"After Cal," Terrence finishes for me.

Olivia had been wrecked about it. Cal died while protecting her. Terrence had been there, too. I know it wasn't easy on any of them. It must have been especially hard on Terrence.

If he weren't driving, I'd pull him into a hug and try to ease his pain. He's obviously still feeling it, and the death of this other friend dredges it all up even more, I suspect.

"Hey, I'm all right," Terrence says.

"I know you are," I say.

He's not mine. I shouldn't worry about him. But all I can picture is sitting somewhere quiet with him and tugging his head into my lap so he can rest and know he's safe and cared for.

Dammit, where is all this coming from?

We don't speak again for a few minutes, but it doesn't feel awkward. Just quiet. Comfortable. After a while, I pull out my phone and check messages. There's a new email from Karl. He wants to get lunch this weekend. I'm about to respond to his note, but I pause, remembering Terrence and Gideon's caution.

"Am I allowed to *talk* to my uncle?" I ask Terrence. "Or is Gideon forbidding me from doing that, too?"

"You can talk to him," Terrence says. "I think it's wisest to avoid seeing him in person until Ironwood can check out more of Gideon's suspicions and see what the story is there."

"The story is that he's my uncle who just wants to have a relationship with his niece," I say.

"Just...see if you can put him off for a bit," Terrence says. "Let us vet him before you give him any trust."

"I think Gideon's being paranoid."

"Noted."

I quickly type out an email to my uncle, telling him I have a few things to take care of over the next few days, but maybe we could grab lunch next week. There. Nice and vague. I don't want him to hear that I don't trust him and that a security company is vetting him, because wow, that's offensive. If I were in his place, I'd be hurt.

Soon, we're in San Esteban and pulling up to my apartment complex.

Terrence waves at someone standing near the entrance. "That's Hunter," he says.

A man with sandy brown hair, wearing jeans and a t-shirt, approaches the car. His eyes are concealed by sunglasses.

"He's a lot less formal than Ironwood guards typically look," I remark.

"We're going to try to blend into your day-to-day life," Terrence says. "In some cases, it's better to be inconspicuous. If your threat rating changes or Ryder and Jaxon disagree with my assessment, we'll adjust accordingly."

I'm glad I won't have multiple suited guards following me around. Hunter looks like a recent graduate from SESA, just like me. He could pose as a buddy.

Terrence pops the trunk, and Hunter immediately goes to it. "The suitcase and the bag?" he asks.

"Yep," Terrence says.

"Thanks," I say.

"No problem." Hunter grabs my things and heads toward the building.

I hesitate. So this is goodbye to Terrence, I guess. A one-night-stand, a random kiss shared in Gideon's kitchen. And Terrence isn't even looking at me.

My emotions are all freakin' over the place. At the moment, I want nothing more than to go into my apartment, clean my room, and hide under my bed for a good cry.

"Look," Terrence says as I start to get out of the car, "I'm not Jaxon or Ryder. I don't share very well. Never have. And while I don't know that I'm in the market for a relationship at the moment, I'm definitely not interested in a love triangle."

Wow, okay, so he isn't holding back. "And you're telling me this because...?" I ask.

"Because I don't want games," he says. "I shouldn't have kissed you earlier. I don't regret it, not in the slightest. But we should probably forget it happened."

"Right," I say. I can't believe this guy. "Consider it forgotten. I've already forgotten."

I've already forgotten. It's a lie. Because as I walk up to my apartment where Hunter is waiting, I can't forget that kiss. As much as I want to, I can't forget anything.

SIXTEEN

Samantha

What I need now is a whole lot of normal. No more of these guys filling my brain with nonsense and super hot sex fantasies. Nope. Back to work, back to my mundane life. I got my room cleaned last night, and Addison even helped me with the laundry, which was sweet and unexpected. I think she feels bad that Greg left the apartment unlocked and mine was the only room that was touched. And Greg gave me all his quarters for laundry.

Maybe, even though they're cheating cheaters who cheated, my roommates aren't entirely bad people?

Nah, I can still hate them while appreciating their help.

Sleeping in my bedroom was a whole other issue.

Feeling squicked out about the invasion of my space, I couldn't settle down, so I ended up sleeping on the couch instead.

So now, it's a relief to be at work. My morning at The Corbin goes by quickly, with reshelving recent returns and then starting a big project with a new cataloging system that will be specific to our library. It's not exactly fun. Tedious, really, but the mental energy it requires makes the time go by faster.

My guards have switched from Hunter, to Roman and then Squid, both of whom I know through Olivia. Now Hunter is back, and he mostly hangs out adjacent to whatever room I'm in. He's either reading or pretending to read. I'm trying not to care that he must be incredibly bored.

It's his job, I remind myself. I get bored with my job a lot, too. Sometimes even when I'm writing smut. Work is work, and we all have to earn a living somehow.

At lunchtime, Izzie offers to take both Millie and me to the deli nearby. The scents of greasy french fries and pesto greet my nose. We order our sandwiches and grab a table, then dig in. Hunter waits outside the crowded deli, peering in at us occasionally through the window, but mostly acting like a rando who can't get off his phone. He's not really paying attention to the phone, though—I can tell he's on high alert, watching for trouble.

"Thanks for joining me today," Izzie says, tucking a strand of her black hair behind her ear. Today, her earrings are made of silver and gold stars dangling from multiple chains. They catch the light every time she moves her head, making her into a human disco ball. "I wanted to thank both of you for all the hard work you're doing. Samantha, I was so relieved you didn't have to take today off, because Will really wants to see that new system happen, sooner rather than later."

Will is one of the co-owners of The Corbin. I've never actually laid eyes on the man, but Izzie talks about him like he's the Godfather or some kind of royalty or something.

"I was glad to make it back this week," I say. Although, if I'd stayed...well, it would be entirely improper to think about what Gideon and I could be doing right this very moment. I shut that thought down, quick.

"And Millie," Izzie says, "you are doing a fantastic job. The Corbin looks better now than it did with our last custodian. Will said he walked through it last night and he was amazed."

"Oh, that's nice to hear," Millie says, flushing slightly.

A couple of tables over, I see a guy I recognize. He's Greg's half-brother. His ice-blue eyes are the same as Greg's, but his hair is light brown instead of blond, and instead of cutting it short, he keeps it shaggy. It takes me a minute to remember his name, but once I do, I wave to get his attention. "Noah, hey!"

His eyes get wide, like he's been caught with his hand in the cookie jar, but he quickly smiles and approaches our table. "Hey, Samantha. How are you?"

"I'm good. Millie, Izzie, this is my friend Noah." *Friend* is maybe too strong a word, because I only met him when Greg, Addison, and I were moving into the apartment—Noah helped us out. Still, we spent hours together that day, and he seemed nice. Quietly funny, in a self-deprecating way.

We exchange hello's all around, then Noah nods awkwardly and says, "I'll just go back to my table now. Good to meet you—"

"Wait, you can join us," Izzie says. Ever the mother hen, she doesn't want to abandon Noah.

"Oh, I couldn't impose," Noah says.

"It's just lunch," I say with a laugh. "Go, get your sandwich."

"He's cute," Izzie whispers as Noah goes to retrieve his food, raising her eyebrows at me.

He seems like a little boy compared to Gideon and Terrence. He's a full-grown, adult man, but I feel zero attraction for the guy. I give Izzie a quick head-shake to let her know she's off-base with the cute comment. She shrugs and winks, like "can't win them all."

Millie and I make space between us at the circular cafe table, and Noah fits a chair into the spot.

"So, I haven't seen you since Greg and Addison

and I moved into the apartment," I say to him. "Are you and Greg on the outs or something?"

"Oh, no, just haven't had the chance to hang out," Noah says, clearing his throat. "I, um, was recently laid off, so I'm busy trying to find a new job."

"Oh, crap, that sucks," I tell him.

"What line of business are you in?" Izzie asks.

"Whatever business I can get," he says. "I'm a renaissance man. Also known as the guy who never declared a major or graduated college."

"Fun, you sound like me," Millie says, holding up her water glass to clink with his, which he does.

"What kinds of interests do you have?" I ask. "Maybe we can think of someone we know who's hiring."

"I love everything," Noah says.

The rest of our lunch break involves Izzie, Millie, and me troubleshooting Noah's employment woes, which is more fun than I would've expected. Then it's back to work, and I'm busy with the new cataloging system. It comprises mostly of data tags, to make certain subtopics easier to find. But wow, it's intense.

My brain is swimming with categories and tags and every possible little bit of metadata that might be used when grouping books together in a database. As I leave the library with Hunter following behind, Cora, another one of Ironwood's bodyguards, approaches from the front.

"Changing of the guards?" I ask.

"Yep," Hunter says. "See you later."

"Hey," Cora says, waving at me. "Are you heading home?"

"Actually, I thought I might hang out in the park nearby. Get some Vitamin D and do a little writing."

"Sure thing," she says. "Lead the way."

We get to the park and I sit at an empty picnic table in the shade. Cora disappears into the trees nearby. I know from past explorations of this park that there's a bench back there, along a trail leading to a playground.

With a happy little hum, I pull my laptop from my bag and turn it on. Soon, I'm lost in Calliope and Alex's story. She needs a bodyguard, he wants to be a boyfriend, he doesn't think he can be both. Calliope, however, needs him to see that both is very, very possible.

The last time I worked on the story, I'd put them in a dance club with Calliope hanging with her friends while Alex acted as her bodyguard.

ALEX WAS NEARBY, guarding her, and so Calliope danced her heart out. Her friends crowded around her, moving to the music. It was deafening, overwhelming. The beat got into her blood.

Song after song, she and her friends danced. When Michael got close to her, his breath heavy on her neck, she allowed it. She'd told him, time and time again, that she didn't have feelings for him, so a bit of sexy dancing would be okay—he knew the score. Their bodies twined together and she felt his hardness against her hip as he clasped her to him.

Better not to push things. She gave Michael a regretful smile and stepped away. He started to follow her, so she put her hand up and shook her head.

He got the message, although he looked disappointed.

Calliope left the dance floor and made her way toward the restrooms. The line was insanely long, but she knew there was another set of restrooms upstairs, so she made her way toward them.

A hand on her wrist stopped her. She nearly screamed in surprise, but his touch was intoxicating—she'd know him anywhere.

"Alex," she breathed.

He leaned down to speak in her ear. "You drive me absolutely fucking crazy, you know that? Everything you do—

"SAMANTHA, IS THAT YOU?" a male voice says, tugging me from the story.

My mood sours. I was in the flow. The scene was going to pour from my fingertips, and now someone is here and I'll have to make conversation.

I look up and see a man approaching. His brown hair is graying at the front and the temples. His mustache is more gray than brown, but it's the same one I recognize from the last time I saw him, years ago.

"Uncle Karl," I say, my voice going high in surprise. "I told you we'd have to set up a lunch date—"

"What can I say," he says, holding out his hands like some kind of circus show-runner. "I couldn't wait to see my favorite niece!"

It's like he expects me to run over and give him a hug or something, but I'm so surprised, I can't seem to stand up.

"Aren't you glad to see me?" he asks.

"Yes, of course," I say, still unable to budge. "This is just unexpected."

From her place a few yards away, Cora is striding toward us, a pissed-off expression on her face. "Sir, you need to leave."

Karl turns to face her. "This is my niece—I'm just saying hello—"

"Sir, I must ask you to step away from Miss Joy."

"But—"

"Sir, I *insist*," she says.

"Samantha," Karl says, his voice pleading. "What's going on?"

"Long story," I say.

He looks at the picnic table. "Well, can I sit and you can tell me about it?"

"Not right now. It's not up to me," I tell him, wincing. My heart feels like it's cracking in my chest. "I told you we could meet later this week after I get some stuff figured out."

He takes one look at me, and then holds his hands up toward Cora in a "no harm" gesture and says, "Okay, Samantha, okay. I'm sorry, you're obviously going through...something. Let me know when you're free."

"I will, I'm so sorry," I tell him while Cora stares him down.

He shakes his head, his shoulders slumped, and walks away defeated.

Cora gives me a shrewd look. "Are you okay?"

"Other than feeling like the world's biggest asshole?" I say.

"Yeah, other than that," she says.

I shake my head. "I feel like the world's biggest asshole. I should go talk to him."

"We're doing some background checks on him, Samantha," Cora says. "There are some red flags, and we just want to make sure he's one hundred percent safe."

"It's not like he's going to draw a gun on me right here in the park," I grumble.

As Cora walks back to her bench, I don't even try to get back into Alex and Calliope's story. I strain my eyes to watch my uncle walk away. He gets smaller and smaller until he disappears.

Samantha

I feel like shit. After Cora walked me home, I ended up vegging out all evening, unable to focus on anything except a medical drama on television.

The next day is Saturday, and I still don't feel like writing. I should've talked to my uncle yesterday, maybe at a distance of several feet apart. I don't know, what do they think he's going to do, hypnotize me into handing over my credit cards or something?

Saturday crawls by. In the evening, Addison and Greg take off—Greg to his job as a bartender, and Addison to go dancing with friends. She opens her mouth like she's considering inviting me, but then she turns around and leaves.

I don't want an invitation, anyway. I want to sulk.

Maybe I don't feel like writing, but writing has to happen, so once they're gone, I open up my manuscript and re-read the scene where I left off yesterday. I'd been so excited about giving my couple a heated, angry kiss in the hallway at the club. I wanted Alex at his breaking point, desperate to touch Calliope, to kiss her.

But as I read over the scene, I frown. Nope, writing isn't going to happen.

Social media. I'll do that. I'm upset about family stuff, so what better way to cheer myself up than checking in with my virtual, online "family" of readers and friends. The Redactible site is bustling, surprisingly popular on a Saturday night. It seems all the other homebodies are here, hanging out. I chat with a few people, and that cheers me up. My readers are looking forward to my next book, which is touching. *Even if it's a hot mess?* I type back to one of them. *Even then*, she writes. *It lets us know you're human.*

I am *so* human. So full of mistakes. Regrets.

And a little bit of anger, too. What the hell does Gideon really think Karl can do to me?

My phone buzzes with a call. Gideon's name lights up the screen. Of course it's him. I debate letting it go to voicemail, but a mixture of curiosity and a desperation to escape this ennui forces me to answer.

"Yeah?" I ask, sounding hostile. Because yeah, I'm still pissed. Even though I miss the stoic old bastard.

"Hey," he says, his voice warm. "I heard there was a thing with Karl yesterday."

"Yep. But my bodyguard chased him off, so don't you worry."

"I'm more worried about your feelings," he says. "Are you all right?"

Ugh. I roll my eyes and look around my empty apartment. "Yeah, I'm fine."

"You're angry."

No use lying about it. "Yep."

"He doesn't even have a job right now," Gideon says. "He's using a fake last name, too."

"So?"

"So he's bad news."

"He's my *only family*," I say.

Gideon is quiet. I wait for him to argue that he, Gideon, is also my family, but if he is, that puts us in a very weird, very awkward situation after everything we did the other night. He's never treated me like a family member, not even when I was a kid. So I'm relieved when he doesn't say anything along those lines now.

"I'm sorry, Sam."

It's my turn to not speak. I don't know what to say.

"Do you want company?" he asks.

I scowl at the apartment door.

"We can talk about the other night," he says.

"If you tell me it was all a mistake and we should forget about it, I swear I will reach through this phone and smack you," I say. Then I stare at my phone, shocked that I just said that out loud. Yikes. But guys pull that shit in romance novels, and it's annoying as fuck. I don't need that in real life.

He laughs. "Just the opposite. I wish you'd stayed here. Clear Springs is lonely without you."

There's sincerity in his voice, and just enough heat to make me sit up and take notice.

I ask, "If I were there, what would we be doing right now?"

"Are you alone?" he asks. "I'll tell you all about it."

Okay, yeah, the way he's talking has me itching to take my clothes off for him. How does he do that?

"I'm alone," I say quietly.

"If you came home right now, I'd take you directly into my office," he says.

"So we can go over my college options?" I ask, snarky.

"No. I'd start off by lifting up your skirt and pulling down your panties. Then I'd bend you over my desk and give you a spanking," he says. "Get that ass warmed up, and remind you who's in charge."

"Would it hurt?"

"A little. Would you like it?"

"Yes," I breathe. Nobody's around. Nobody has to know I'm easing my free hand down into my panties. My fingers meet the slippery wetness of my arousal.

"Would it help remind you that I'm in charge?"

"Uh-huh."

"Tell me," he says.

"Tell you?"

"Tell me who's in charge."

"You're in charge, Gideon," I say, and even though I'm giving him control, I've never felt freer.

"Good job," he says, and the praise warms me through and through. "Now put the phone on speaker so you can use both your hands to do everything I tell you."

Terrence

Samantha's apartment door is thin. Her voice is soft, but I can hear her words, intermixed with Gideon's. I know she's alone in there, so they must be on the phone.

I should've never offered to take Roman's shift.

And yet I can't seem to pull myself away.

SEVENTEEN

Terrence

I lean my head back against the door. I can hear far too much from inside Samantha's apartment.

"Well?" Gideon says. His voice isn't quite as clear as Samantha's, because it's coming through her phone, but I can still make out his words. "Tell me what you're wearing."

"A skirt," she says.

"And under your skirt?"

"Pink underwear."

"I bet they're wet," he says.

Her voice is faint. "So wet."

I step away from the door and lean against the wall. Fuck. If she wants to have sex, she doesn't need to settle for some voice over the phone. I'm right fucking here, Samantha. My dick is hard and ready, and I could fuck away your lust, satisfy you again and again until you beg me to give you a break.

But I'm working. I gotta clear my head, not creep on the client. That's what she is—a client. This is a job.

Their voices seep through the wall, but away from the door, I can't hear the actual words.

I shouldn't listen.

But it's late. Nearing eleven. No one else is around, the open corridor is empty.

Unable to help myself, I move next to the door again.

"And when I'm in charge," he says, "what do you call me?"

There's a pause, and I imagine Samantha's brow wrinkling while she thinks. "Sir?"

"*Sir* works," he says.

She's a natural submissive, I could tell that much in our short time together. She called me *Sir* in Hawaii and I nearly came on the spot. I had to change our position up to give myself a breather.

"Oh, good, because I really wasn't sure about *Master*," Samantha says.

"If I wanted you to call me *Master,* would you?"

Another pause, and then Samantha says, "Yes."

"Yes, what?"

"Yes, Sir."

"Good girl."

"Oh, fuck," she says. "Why does that turn me on so much?"

He laughs quietly. "Does it turn you on more or less than my tongue at your pussy?"

"Mmm," she moans. "Slightly less."

"Are you touching your little cunt right now? You should be."

"I am," she says.

I picture that—Samantha on a bed. No, she's probably in the living room on a couch, with her dress bunched up around her waist, her panties shoved to the side. No, her panties completely off, giving her unrestricted access to her pussy. There's a look of pleasured concentration on her face as she fingers herself and rubs her clit. Her phone is on the couch next to her, with Gideon's voice coming from it, ordering her around.

"Take your fingers away from your cunt," Gideon orders.

"What? No, it feels too good," she says.

"You better listen to me, you naughty thing," he says, "or I'll come down there and give you a spanking you won't soon forget."

"Promise?" she asks.

He growls in frustration. "Fingers away from your cunt, now, or I hang up."

"Okay, okay! I stopped."

I'm tempted to kick down her door and go in and make sure she's telling the truth. Mischievous little minx wouldn't hesitate to tell him what he wants to hear while she continues doing exactly what she wants.

But she says, "Really, Sir, I stopped. Please...tell me what to do next?"

"That's my precious girl," he says.

No, I think. She's *my* precious girl.

Yet as jealous as I am listening to this, I'm just as turned on.

"Now, lift up your shirt, and tell me about your tits," Gideon says. "I want to be sucking on those little nipples. Are they covered in a bra right now?"

"Yes, Sir. Should I take it off?"

"No. Pull down the bra cups," he says. "Tell me—are those nipples hard yet, or do they need extra sucking?"

"They're hard," she says. "But I want you to suck them anyway."

"If I were there, I'd be sucking *and* biting them."

"I wish you were here," she whimpers.

I know the expression she's wearing right now, the way she would be watching me—no, him—as he lowers his face to her chest. I know how she'd slide her legs together, pressing her thighs against each other to relieve that ache that's growing in her pussy. I've watched her do it, and fuck, I want to watch her do it again.

"Pinch them for me," Gideon says. "Are you doing it?"

"I'm—yes, oh fuck, yes, I'm doing it," she says.

"Good girl. Now do it harder."

"Gideon—"

"Sir."

"Sir—ow, it hurts—"

"Excellent," he says. "Now think about doing this, with me."

"That's all I can think about," she says.

"With me," he says, then pauses. "With me, and with someone else watching you."

"Someone?"

"Anyone," he says in a lower, quieter voice.

Fucking hell, I can't believe I'm getting to hear this. My submissive exhibitionist, talking out a scene with another dominant.

"Anyone," Samantha echoes.

"Maybe the bodyguard. Terrence."

I feel like I'm choking, I'm so turned on, this could kill me.

He continues, "I'm sucking on your tits and fingering you. He's standing to the side, unable to look away. Go ahead, precious girl, and finger that pretty cunt while you play with your tits. I'm doing these things, and he's watching."

"Oh my god," Samantha says. "Yes—yes."

"Are you going to come, Sam?"

"Yeah. Yes, I am, Sir, please, *please*."

"You can come," he says. "I want to hear it, though."

I want to be in there so fucking bad, but instead I'm stuck out here as her bodyguard. This is torture. It would take more willpower than I possess to step away.

So my forehead rests against Samantha's door while she lets out a breathy cry of delight, her voice shaking as her orgasm shudders through her.

Fuck. This job, this girl—it's going to kill me.

Before Samantha, if I was horny, I'd go to Low Vice, the BDSM version of Margot's dance club. But the thought of doing a scene with a stranger doesn't appeal. Nor does dancing with a stranger at Vice.

Has this girl ruined me for everyone else? I'm fucked.

Gideon

I've jacked off twice more since last night's phone sex with Samantha. The girl's in my blood, in my mind.

She's in my heart.

My office feels obscenely empty today. The whole house feels obscenely empty. Times like this, I start to wish I worked from an actual office, a place full of people. Then I remember, I hate people. I'd much rather be alone.

There's one person I want, though.

So I text her. *What are you doing today?*

Working, she responds.

At the Corbin?

No, I'm writing today.

I'm about to ask for some details, wondering what

kind of erotic, romantic drama she's crafting, when a notification pops up, telling me I have a new email from Sammie Starr.

I rush to open the email, expecting a download link for a new book. Instead, there's a bunch of text.

Samantha has sent me her draft. *This is incomplete*, she's written at the top. *Still in progress. But if you're bored enough to harass me while I'm trying to write, maybe this can keep you busy for a little while.*

The girl is practically begging to be spanked, sassing me like this. But I'm too eager to read what she's sent, so I'll deal with her brattiness later.

Settling into my desk chair, I sit back and read. The story follows a woman and her bodyguard.

A bodyguard, huh? I wonder if Sam's real-life experience with Terrence inspired the character.

This story is what I was reading on her laptop the other night. The bodyguard was worried about preying on the heroine...sort of like I've been fearing that I'm doing to Samantha. She's so much younger than me, hell, it feels like it should be wrong.

It's not wrong. It can't be wrong. My feelings for her are real, and they aren't just lust and desire...there's genuine care and acceptance, too. I know her. I *know* her. Better than anyone, probably.

Better than some bodyguard, like Terrence.

The bodyguard in the story is torn between pursuing the heroine and keeping his professional distance. I wonder if Terrence is experiencing a similar battle. That kiss I saw between them in the kitchen on Thursday, that wasn't nothing. He still wants her. How could he not? I almost pity the poor asshole.

Samantha seems to like being watched. I wonder if that could be arranged somehow, with him. I could watch the two of them fuck—no, to hell with that. I'll do her while *he* watches, just like I told her last night on the phone.

It's not going to happen anyway; it's all just fantasy and fiction.

Speaking of fiction, I have an unfinished manuscript to read. So I allow myself to be pulled into the story. There are holes in it—skipped lines where Samantha is doubtlessly going to fill in description or entire plot points. She left notes to herself in all-caps throughout, like, *REMEMBER WHAT HE LOOKS LIKE* and *HERE'S A GOOD SPOT TO SET UP THE FRIENDSHIP W/ MICHAEL*. But despite those notes reminding me I'm not reading the full, finished product, I still fall under the author's spell.

Sammie Starr. My little Samantha.

Come home, I text.

I am home, she texts back.

It's an order. That's a long shot, but it's worth a try.

I'm not taking orders at this time.

Shit.

If she won't come to me, then I'll come to her. It only takes me two minutes to gather my wallet and keys and get behind the wheel.

I drive myself because it's Clay's day off. The two-hour drive goes surprisingly quickly, maybe because my mind is full of Samantha. I try to push thoughts of her away and replace them with thoughts of the marketing firm, but it's impossible. I think about that scene from her book, the one in the club where Alex finally snaps and drags Calliope away, back to his apartment, where they fuck over and over again, wildly, without any thought, both of them slaves to their lust.

That's how it was with Samantha the other night at my house. I couldn't stop claiming her, over and over again. I was like a fucking teenager. Scenes from that night replay in my mind, interspersed with the scene she described when she was with Terrence, how he raced after her, captured her against the bed. Fuck, I'd love to watch that, it would be so hot to watch him take her, demand that her body bend to his will.

When I get to her place, will she let me in? She didn't want to take orders over the phone. She might not even open the door for me.

I don't care. If she doesn't allow me in, that's fine, that's her decision. I'll leave. I just miss her so damn much, I have to try.

I pull up to Samantha's building and start looking for a parking spot. As I yank on the emergency brake, though, a familiar man moves across the parking lot. Terrence. He sees me and stops.

He's probably here to guard Samantha. That's all. Her protection is literally his job.

I hold up a hand to wave and get out of my car.

"Here for work?" I ask, trying to sound casual and not like I need to punch him in the face for daring to think about Samantha the same way I'm thinking about her.

He gives me a hard look. "Sort of."

Shit. So he's not here for work. I didn't expect this kind of complication. I expected Samantha to be the one to put a stop to this madness...not Terrence. But here he is.

She probably called him here. She should—he's much better for her than I am.

I start to get back in my car.

"You're leaving already?" he says.

"Just remembered there's somewhere else I need to be," I say.

He doesn't buy it, but he doesn't try to argue with me, either. I'm old, I've got at least a decade on him, and more than that on Samantha. I shouldn't even be here, despite my all-consuming desire to defile Samantha.

"All right, man," he says. He opens his mouth to add something, but seems to think twice and snaps his mouth shut again. Then he asks, "You want me to tell her I saw you?"

"No, don't mention it, thanks." This is fucking

embarrassing. I'm like a seventh grader, biking past my crush's house and hoping her family doesn't see me.

Terrence nods. Maybe we're competing for Samantha, but there's a kinship between us despite that rivalry. Or maybe because of it.

EIGHTEEN

Samantha

It's around noon on Sunday, and Greg and Addison are having one of those subtle, tense arguments in the kitchen. Nobody's raising their voice, but the conflict and discomfort is palpable.

Ugh, I need to not have roommates anymore. I'm trying to write joyful sexy times between two enthusiastically consenting adults, but that's hard to do when the nearest couple is giving off "I'm going to smother you tonight and not in the fun way" vibes.

Sighing inwardly, I don my noise-cancelling headphones and turn on a "calming beats" playlist. I return my focus back to my screen and the little words crawling across the white backdrop of the document.

. . .

"BEND OVER, sweetheart, and show me what's mine," Alex said.

Calliope frowned. "That's not very romantic."

"There's nothing romantic about tonight," he said. "This is going to be filthy and fast and you're going to love it."

With that, Alex spun Calliope around and pushed her back down, effectively making her bend over.

Bent to his will, she held in a moan. His hand cupped her pussy, heat and faint friction. She wanted more. She needed more.

YES, okay. I can get into this scene, no problem. I wonder how the flavor would change if another man were there with them. Like, what if Calliope's friend Michael is more than a friend? What if he follows them to the apartment, and all three of them...? No, that's not the story I'm writing.

But there's no denying it's on my mind as I brainstorm what the hero and heroine are about to do next.

I have a few ideas.

No sooner do my fingers come down on the keyboard, before Addison waves to get my attention from across the room. I lift one ear of my headphones.

"There's someone at the door for you," she says, pointing.

I turn sideways and jolt at the sight of Terrence standing there, then hurry to turn off my music and remove my headphones. "Terrence, hey, come on in. Unless you're guarding me right now...?"

"Guarding?" Addison asks.

"Long story," I say.

Terrence shakes his head. "I'm not on duty, but I want to talk to you."

"Tell me about the guarding," Addison says. "Is that who that woman was, hanging around our hall when I came home? Was she a guard, or is she stalking you or something?"

"She's a bodyguard, and I'm not going to get into the story right now," I say.

Frowning in a mixture of frustration and concern, Addison flips her hair over her shoulder and returns to the kitchen, where she and Greg continue whatever argument they were having.

Terrence looks around my apartment with interest. "Nice place."

I try to see it through his eyes. The second-hand sofa that I tried, unsuccessfully, to cover up with a colorful throw blanket and pillows. Addison's paintings from SESA, which are all blotchy shapes in monochrome black and gray. The beer cans Greg never remembers to take to the recycling bin. This place isn't nice, but it's nice of Terrence to say so.

"You should've thought of that before you looked twice at that bitch," Addison says in a raised voice.

Greg responds, "I wouldn't have if you paid any attention to me at all!"

I look at Terrence. "Um, should we go for a walk or something?"

He nods, looking relieved. "Yeah."

It's noon, in the middle of August, so I don't grab a sweater, I just slide on a pair of flip-flops and head outside in my shorts and tank top. Terrence is in jeans and a black t-shirt, somehow exuding a hot bodyguard aura without even trying.

Roman, who's been hanging out against the railing outside of my apartment, looking down into the courtyard below, nods at me. "Should I come with you two?"

"Nah, you can take a break," Terrence says.

"Cool," Roman says. "Send me a text when you're back, or if you need me to meet you somewhere else."

Terrence and I agree, then we head down the stairs to the sidewalk. We walk along the street. We're headed in the direction of a park-turned-nature preserve that borders San Esteban. I sometimes walk here when I need to think out tricky issues with my plots or characters. It's an odd little oasis in what oftentimes feels like a crowded, big city.

"So," I say. "What's up?"

"A couple of things," Terrence says.

"Okay." I keep walking, not willing to press for answers. He came to me, so if he wants to talk, that's up to him.

"First off," he says, "is the work-related item. Karl Jeffries."

"My uncle." I take in a deep breath, preparing for

what Terrence might tell me. Whatever he says, I can take it, but I hope Karl's okay. "What did Ironwood find out about him? He's fine, right?"

Shaking his head, Terrence says, "He's bad news, Samantha. Gideon was right."

"Bad news, how?"

"We don't know why, exactly, but he's using a false last name, and there's no employment record for either this name or his other one. So we believe this is one of several aliases."

"That doesn't necessarily mean he wants my money," I say.

"Samantha," Terrence says, his brown eyes soft. "He's a con artist. He definitely wants your money."

I shake my head. What would my uncle need with my money? When I saw him at the park, he looked happy and well-to-do. I think back, searching for details or clues. He had on nice clothes, nice shoes. Everything about him was polished, and the only vibe I got off of him was that of disappointment when I wouldn't let him sit down for a chat.

"He just wants to talk to me," I say.

"He's going to spin you a tale," Terrence says. "Ironwood isn't going to punish you if you go against our recommendation of no contact with him. But Gideon might. Then again, you might like Gideon's punishment."

"Shut up," I say, my cheeks feeling warm with a blush.

He takes my hand and his fingers are strong and warm against mine. "I'm serious, though. The guy is bad news. Keep within sight of your bodyguard at all times, okay?"

"Yeah, okay." I want to lean against him, borrow his strength, take comfort from him. But he isn't mine, and I don't know what's allowed between us.

We've reached the wooded nature preserve when I remember—"You said there are a couple of things you wanted to talk about?"

"Yes," he says. "The second one is about the other day, at Gideon's house. I kissed you, and I can't stop thinking about it."

If I'm honest, it's been on my mind, too, as much as I try to shove it away. I'd been so embarrassed, yet also a little...turned on? When Gideon walked in and wasn't mad, it made me think of all the things he'd said the night before, and how fucking arousing it all was. I'd been kissing one guy while another guy watched.

It reminded me a little of this time when I was in college, my first year. I'd known someone was watching from the shadows while my date and I had gotten each other off against the side of the dorms. It had been such a turn-on, knowing someone was witnessing my pleasure. Honestly, the guy I was with barely knew what he was doing. I think I didn't get off because of anything he did, but because of the person hiding in the shadows, watching.

"Samantha?" Terrence says.

"Yeah, the kiss." I blink up at him. "I can't stop thinking about it, either. Or that night in Hawaii. But you said it would only be the one time, so I've been trying to ignore those thoughts."

He steers us toward a trail that leads into a wood of older trees. The trunks are thicker, and it's cooler here, more private. In fact, I haven't seen anyone else in quite some time. After the tension-soaked arguments in my apartment, this feels peaceful and quiet.

"Maybe it should've been only the one time," Terrence says, frowning and rubbing his goatee.

Okay, now he's talking nonsense. "Then why are you here?"

"Because I can't stop thinking about you. I'm messed up, Samantha. But I still want to see you, and I don't think I can keep myself from coming to you again and again. I mean, fuck, look at me here with you now. It's not my shift for guard duty, but I couldn't resist. If I didn't come to tell you about your uncle, I would've found some other excuse."

I stop walking and face him. "So tell me what you want."

"I want to be with you," he says. "And I know you're seeing Gideon, or maybe it's more casual than that. But I wish I was him. I wish you were seeing me."

"So, you want to fuck around," I say.

He steps closer to me. "Yeah, I guess that's the idea."

"Is this a no-strings kind of proposition? Because I don't think I can be exclusive."

"Because of Gideon," he says.

I wince. "Yeah. Is that going to be a problem?"

"How about...only Gideon. And me. But nobody else."

As there isn't anyone else on my radar, this is sounding good. Except... "I don't think I could be so generous," I say. "If we're starting a relationship, even if it's solely based on sex, the thought of you with another person is just...I can't."

His brown eyes bore into mine. "I don't want anyone else."

"I feel bad. I wish I could say the same, but there's Gideon. I want him, too."

"I don't feel bad," he says. "It works for me. You'll have to make sure it works for him, too. You can think about it, if you want. And who says the relationship will just be based on sex?"

"I don't know, I don't want to make any assumptions," I say.

"I'm making an assumption right now," he says, his voice going low. He looks meaningfully at me, and then at the very empty trail where we stand.

If my arousal were a cat, its ears would be perking up right now, and its pupils dilating with interest.

"Yeah?" I say. "What are you assuming?"

"I don't know if I should tell you."

I laugh. "Tell me! Come on, you can't just say

you're making an assumption and not tell me what it is."

"I can do whatever I want," he says. "But sure, I'll tell you. My assumption is that you want my hand in your panties."

Taking a step back, I say, "Maybe I do. But you're going to have to catch me to find out."

He leans back in surprise. Then a smile grows on his face as he looks around at the empty area. "You better run, baby. Because if I catch you, I'm not letting you go."

I'm wearing freaking flip-flops, but whatever. I'm not going to get far—this won't be much of a chase. But I'll do anything for that smile of his, the lustful approval I can see in his beautiful eyes.

Taking a deep breath, I spin around and dart away from him.

He doesn't chase me immediately. Confident bastard. Maybe I'll actually escape this time. The idea that I could get away gives me a thrill. What kind of twisted game is this, anyway?

The trail leads away from the main part of the nature preserve. I have to run carefully so I don't fall down. The trail isn't super well-maintained and I get the impression people don't come back here often.

From behind me, quick footfalls thud against the dirt.

He's chasing me.

I keep moving, and I'm not sure how long I run for.

It's getting harder to suck in air. I should start working out of this whole chasing game is going to be a thing between us. After a few minutes, my legs begin to ache, and my lungs protest every breath. Yeah, I definitely need to do more cardio.

He's still behind me—I can hear him.

Holy hell, I want to get away but I want to get caught at the same time. Why should I make it easy for him, though? I risk a look over my shoulder. Terrence isn't in sight—he gave me a good head start. He probably wants to make the chase last longer, the smug bastard. Well, I can help him with that. I put on a burst of speed, still careful of my stupid shoes. Then I dart off the side of the trail.

A few feet into the shadows, and I lean against a large trunk. I keep to the side facing away from the trail. I clap a hand over my mouth to keep my heavy breaths from sounding too loudly.

He runs past, and I let go of my mouth. Ha. Take that, you big bossy bodyguard. I can run *and* hide.

His running footsteps halt a few yards down the trail. "Sneaky little girl," he mutters, then backtracks.

I peer around the edge of the trunk. Through the thick foliage, I can see his legs, but not his face or chest.

Without warning, he plows into the brush, coming right at me.

Shit. He's not far away. I could stay here and hope to hide from him, or I can take off again. My legs ache and I'm tempted to stay put. But adrenaline forces me to bolt.

"There you are," he says, a mocking note in his voice.

Not thinking about anything except getting away, I speed up. The toe of my flip-flop catches on a rock. I fall forward, catch myself on a tree trunk. The impact isn't bad, but before I can recover and take off again, a large arm comes around my waist, imprisoning me against a rock-hard body.

"Gotcha," he whispers in my ear.

He pushes me against a tree so I'm facing the wood, my hands up to brace myself. He covers my body with his. If anyone were to wander into this overgrown wooded area, they wouldn't be able to see what we're doing.

And what we're doing is, in a word, incredible. He unsnaps the buttons of my jean shorts and shoves his hand down the front of my panties. I'm already wet, and as soon as his fingers make contact with my pussy, I'm drenched. I want his cock, not his fingers, but we're in public—even this is too much.

Too much, yet not enough. That seems to describe every moment with these guys.

"Terrence," I gasp.

"Call me *Sir*," he says, his breath hot on my neck. "I caught you, I earned your respect."

Oh, fuck yes. It reminds me of my phone call with

Gideon the other night. And I called Terrence *Sir* when we were in Hawaii.

"Yes, Sir," I say, losing myself in the decadent, impossibly pleasurable feeling of his callused fingers manipulating my clit.

He bites my shoulder, right over the faint redness left over from Gideon's mark. I had to wear higher-necked t-shirts for the last few days to keep anyone from seeing that. Looks like I'll have to do some more laundry and replenish my supply of those shirts.

Thoughts of laundry fly from my brain as he kisses and licks the mark, lashing his tongue over it, the whiskers of his goatee abrading my skin.

My orgasm is close. My feet flex and I try to rise up on my tiptoes, chasing the pressure of Terrence's fingertips.

"Please, please," I whisper.

"Are you close, baby?" he asks.

"Yes, Sir. Please, I'm so close."

"Give me your orgasm," he says. "Come on my fingers. Right now, baby, you can do it."

There's no stopping it. I cry out briefly before remembering we're in a semi-public place, then I choke it down, gasping as ecstasy tears through me.

"There you go," he says. "Just what you needed, wasn't it?"

I can barely move, but he turns me around so I face him. He kisses my shoulder again over the place where he bit me and smiles. "The mark won't last...this time."

Is it weird I'm disappointed by that? Even stranger is the image that pops into my head of a bite mark on each shoulder, one from Gideon, one from Terrence.

He helps put me to rights, straightening my tank and buttoning up my shorts, while my brain whirls with ideas. Olivia has two boyfriends. Husbands, now. But they started out together, Jaxon and Ryder. When they met Olivia, they'd already been friends and they knew they liked sharing women. It's too bad I can't get that with Gideon and Terrence.

The idea is tantalizing, though. This would be a lot less confusing, too, if they came as a set.

Terrence's phone chirps in his pocket and he takes it out, frowning at the screen. "I have to go in to Ironwood," he says. "I'll walk you back to your place, first."

"Sure," I say. "Is everything all right?"

"Yeah. Issues with another client. Ryder and Jaxon will be back soon to deal with all this shit. In the meantime, it falls on Leonie and me."

Terrence

I call Roman back to Samantha's apartment and leave her under his capable watch. I don't want to leave her at all, but Jaxon and Ryder put me in charge of guarding issues, while Leonie is running the tech division.

As I'm leaving Samantha's place, I catch a glimpse of a man standing across the street. He has gray-brown hair and a mustache. His face is partially obscured by a baseball cap and he's wearing sunglasses, but I've pored over enough photos of the guy to recognize him anywhere.

Karl Jeffries.

The asshole needs to take the hint and leave Samantha alone.

I text Roman. *Jeffries is across the street. Be alert.*

He texts me back a thumb's up.

I walk back to my car, hating that I have to go into the office. Maybe it wouldn't hurt to put a second guy on Samantha.

NINETEEN

Terrence

A few days go by, and I'm so busy with Ironwood, I don't have a chance to do much more than check in with Samantha via text. Finally, I can't stand it anymore. I have to see her. Our brief time in the woods was exactly that—brief. Not enough.

The parking lot behind the Corbin is reserved for paying members of the library, so I park on the street a block away. As I'm walking up to the library from one end of the block, I see a familiar figure coming toward the library from the other end.

It can't be him.

Fuck me, it *is* him—it's Gideon. Our strides bring us to the library steps at the same time, where we stop and face each other.

"Again?" he says. "Or are you here for Ironwood?"

"I'm here for Samantha."

"I'm not running off this time," he says. "I drove all this way to see her, so I'm going to see her."

"That's fine," I say.

"I don't need your permission."

No, he doesn't. Dude looks like he'd throw a punch if I argued with him. I can't imagine it's easy for him, living two hours away from her. Hell, I'm only twenty minutes away during heavy traffic, and that seems too far.

I shouldn't be so fucking smitten with her, and yet, here I am, surprising her at her place of work just because I want to say hello.

Too bad Gideon is here, too. If I were a nice guy, I'd leave, let him have a few moments with her.

But I'm not a nice guy. I'm here for her, and I won't let anyone stop me.

We shoulder in through the double doors at the same time. I don't shove Gideon, but it's tempting, and our bodies knock together as we go. He shoots me a disgruntled look, which I return.

As we stumble into the library, it's Samantha who stands at the front desk. Several yards away from her, Cora is leaning against the doorway to another room, pretending to read a book while on guard duty. She sees Gideon and I the moment we step through the door, of course, and there's a faint smirk on her face.

Yeah, it's real fucking amusing, me competing with another guy for Samantha's affections.

"Gideon?" Samantha says. "Terrence? What are you both doing here?"

"I came to say hi," I say, at the same time Gideon says, "I'm here for you—I wanted to see you."

A pleased smile forms on her face. "Well, hello to you both. This is a surprise, a good surprise."

It would be a better surprise if Gideon hadn't shown up to spoil it, but fine. "Is your day going all right?" I ask her.

"Yeah, it's fine," she says. "Just busy. Izzie had to take a couple hours off so I'm taking care of the circulation desk."

Just then, the phone rings. Holding up a finger to tell us to wait, Samantha answers it. "Corbin Library... no, this is a privately owned and operated library." A pause. "Of course, yes. For things like that, you'll want the public library." She recites a phone number, then hangs up and turns back to us. "I keep getting phone calls, so I can't really chat right now."

"Can I take you to lunch?" Gideon asks, leaning against the counter.

"I was going to ask you out to lunch." I knock his elbow from the counter with mine.

In retaliation, he knocks my arm back off and takes up the entire side of the counter with his broad shoulders.

"Guys," Samantha says in a sharp voice. "What are you going to do next, rock-paper-scissors?"

Gideon and I look at each other. The expression on his face matches my own thoughts—it isn't a bad idea.

Samantha waves us away. "I'm at work. Call, text, email, chat me on Redactible, I don't care. You have lots of options. But coming here to my place of work and then bickering over me like two boys fighting over a bike? Not cool. I'm not going to lunch with either of you today."

I want to put her over my knee for that impertinence, but there's no arguing with her point, because she's right.

Also, I'm here for her, and I told myself I wouldn't let anyone stop me. But one person can stop me: Samantha. Dammit.

I nod. "I'll call you, and we can set something up."

"And I'll do the same," Gideon says.

"I miss you both." Samantha bites her lower lip, looking vulnerable and sexy and a little unsure. "I'll be looking forward to your calls."

I wish I could lean forward, cup her cheek in my hand, and press a kiss to those luscious lips of hers. But she's working, and I don't want to cause her any problems.

Gideon looks like he feels the same as the two of us turn away from her and leave the library. I carefully avoid looking at Cora, who's probably laughing at me.

When Gideon and I get out onto the front steps, by some unspoken agreement, we both stop.

"I'm suddenly free for lunch," Gideon says, a challenging grin on his face. "And I know you're available. Want to grab a bite?"

The best answer would probably be no, but the truth is, he doesn't seem like a bad guy. Just because we're both pursuing Samantha, doesn't mean we need to be enemies.

"Yeah, all right," I say.

We walk up the street to an upscale pizza place, where we order a pie and a couple of beers.

"So," Gideon says, "how'd you get into the security business?"

"A family friend owned a firm when I was growing up. He got me started while I was still in high school. Not in protection, of course, but working in the office, that sort of thing. I got to sit in on meetings where they came up with schematics, and I got to work out in the company gym with the older guys." I shrug. "As the business grew up, so did I, and eventually I took on guarding responsibilities."

"Do you like it?"

"I guess so." Except when my friends die. I don't like it at all, then. "How about you? You're in...marketing?"

"Yeah. I started the firm with Sam's dad, Matt. I like it. Loved it, when Matt was a part of it, too. Have you ever lost a friend?"

"Yeah, I have." I take a long swig of beer. I didn't expect the conversation to get so personal, so fast. Maybe Gideon's trying to get to know his enemy.

He seems to understand I don't want to talk details. "It changes you. At least it changed me. Changed my whole life. When Matt and Cassie died, I was suddenly responsible for their daughter. And I did a shit job of it."

"She turned out great, though," I point out.

"Yeah, no thanks to me," he says, sounding bitter.

A server brings our pizza over and we dig in. I imagine what it would be like if Samantha were with us, sitting in this booth. Would she sit next to me, or Gideon? Or would he and I sit next to each other so we could make eye contact with her more easily? I think I'd want to sit next to her, rest my hand on her knee, maybe tease her a little.

"You're thinking about her now," Gideon says.

"All the time."

"Same."

We're quiet for a moment, although now that we're getting food in our stomachs, we're no longer eating like starving teenagers.

"I have a confession," Gideon says.

I wait, unsure of where this is going, and whether I want to know.

He says, "We talk about you sometimes. It turns her on to imagine you watching."

I can't help smiling at the thought. "She's an exhibitionist, that's for sure."

"So you don't mind," he says.

"Nah. Whatever gets her off. Besides, I like the thought that she's thinking of me when she's with you."

He snorts. "Asshole."

"Pretty much," I say. "I want her, and I'm not going to pretend otherwise."

"Same here. I'm not pretending any longer with her. I've wasted years."

"Years, huh? You're not a pedo or anything...?"

"Fuck, *no*," he says. "I mean, since she left for college, she's sent me things that...yeah. She's been teasing me for years now. Since she was an *adult*, okay?"

"Okay, I get it," I say, although I don't, not entirely. Has Samantha been sending him nudes or something? Whatever, not my business. I need to focus on winning her now, not five years ago. "All right, we're cool?"

He shrugs and takes a sip of his beer. "Yep. We can both pursue her at the same time. She can decide who she wants to spend her time with."

"Right," I say. "May the best man win."

He laughs. "I'll send you condolence flowers."

"Don't bother. I'll be too busy with Samantha's sweet body to smell any roses."

Chuckling, we knock our nearly-empty pints together, pay the bill, and go our separate ways. He's not a bad guy, I suppose. If we didn't have to fight for Samantha, we'd probably be friends.

Samantha

A few days have gone by, and I still don't have any clear answers about my uncle. Nobody seems to know anything, whenever I talk to my bodyguards. I really just want to talk to Karl, get the story from him, but I don't know whether that's wise.

I go to lunch with Gideon one day, and Terrence the next. They're smarter about this now, arranging dates in advance, almost like they're trying not to step on each other's toes. It makes it easier for me to enjoy myself, that I'm not worried about them getting into a pissing contest.

A part of me misses that little thrill I got when Gideon walked in on Terrence and me kissing. It had been mortifying in some ways, but also...kinda hot.

It's Sunday, and I don't have work, and I don't have plans with either of the guys.

What I do have is another email from Uncle Karl.

HI, Samantha,

You can tell me to buzz off if you want, but I just want to try one last time to get in touch. It seems there's a lot going on for you. Here's my phone number in case you want to reach out. I'm your family and I'll help you with anything you need. I hope I'm not overstepping.

Love,
Uncle Karl

THAT'S IT. I need to put this thing to rest and find out once and for all whether my possibly-a-con-artist uncle has dire plans for my trust fund. Terrence said I can talk to him, after all, just to keep my bodyguard in sight at all times. That's doable.

If he asks me for money, I'm out.

I type the number from the bottom of his email into my phone, then send a text.

Hey, it's Samantha.

His response comes quickly. *Samantha! I'm so relieved to hear from you. Are you in some kind of trouble?*

I hope not. If you want to catch up, I'm free today.

I could do that, he writes back. *Where and when?*

Somewhere public, where my bodyguard won't lose sight of me. Somewhere familiar, so I feel safe. I've never felt like Uncle Karl was a danger to me, but the whole Ironwood plan of protection or whatever it's called, keeps me from being cavalier about this.

There's a coffee shop at the university, near the Cassiopeia building. Meet me there in a half-hour?

I'll be there.

After throwing on some jeans and a nice top, I grab my bag and meet my bodyguard outside my apartment. It's Hunter right now.

"Hey, I'm going to meet my uncle in a few minutes. I wanted to give you a head's up."

"I appreciate it," he says, putting his sunglasses on top of his sandy hair so I can see his eyes. "Are you meeting in a public place?"

"Yeah. A coffee shop on the SESA campus."

"All right, let's go."

It isn't a long walk, so we go on foot. My uncle is already there when we arrive. He gives Hunter a concerned look and holds out his arms. "Am I allowed to hug my favorite niece?"

"I'm your only niece," I say with a smile, stepping into his embrace. He smells like aftershave and laundry detergent and I wrinkle my nose, trying not to sneeze on his shoulder.

I pull away and jerk my head toward the counter. "Should we get some drinks?"

"Sure," he says, grinning.

Once we have coffees in front of us—coffees that *he* pays for, not me—we give each other a good look. My uncle's hazel eyes are similar in shade to my mom's, if the photos I have of her are anything to go by. More striking is their shape—very round, like he's always surprised. My mother's were the same way. I used to wish my eyes were bigger and rounder like theirs, for a connection to my family. I'd walk around

Gideon's giant house, holding my eyes open as wide as I could.

"It's hard to believe you're all grown up," Uncle Karl says, his smile wide beneath his mustache. He points to the way my fingers tap at my iced coffee cup. "Did you know, your mother used to drum her fingers on cups exactly the same way?"

"Really?" I ask, looking down at my fingers. Unlike wishing for round eyes, this isn't something I do consciously.

"Yeah." He gives me another fond smile. "It used to drive our mom, your nana, absolutely nuts."

I laugh, vaguely remembering Nana. She wanted everything just so. I had to wear fancy dresses and let my mom curl my hair before she came to visit. It was awful.

"What else can you tell me about my mom?" I ask.

"Hmm. Well, she played softball in high school. She was the pitcher—she was really good."

I know this, because I have her old yearbooks. "Did she love it, or was it just, you know...she was good at it so she felt she had to do it?"

"She loved it," Uncle Karl says. "I got dragged to all her games because I was younger and didn't have my driver's license yet. And she'd be just...jubilant after a game. Even on the rare occasion her team lost. The sport energized her."

Wow. Now this is the kind of stuff a yearbook can't tell me.

"What else?" I ask.

He goes through a few more tidbits about my mom. I hadn't realized I was so hungry for these details, but they're fueling me while also making me want more. I never got to know her like this, as a person, as someone who had a life before I was born. It's absolutely incredible.

The conversation winds down, and our drinks are nearly empty.

"Sorry, I monopolized the conversation with Mom," I say. "How are you? What are you up to in San Esteban?"

"Oh, I'm consulting on a building project."

"Really? You're in...what, construction?"

"Architecture," he says.

"Cool."

"Yeah, I enjoy it. Not the same way your mom loved softball, but we can't all follow our passions." He smiles ruefully, then brightens. "Career Day at the high school was an event for her—you should've seen her."

"Yeah?"

He checks his watch and his round eyes get even rounder. "Oh, shit—pardon my French. I have to head out."

"Oh, already?" My shoulders fall. I want that story about Career Day.

"Sadly, yes. I've been subletting a place downtown, a nice little apartment," he says. "The sublet's almost up, though, and soon I'll be kicked out. I have to get a new place. Maybe outside San Esteban, because there's not a lot available here."

"Aw, are you going to leave town already?" I ask. I'd give anything for more stories about my mom—I'm not ready for him to take off so soon.

"Well, unless a miracle happens, I'll have to."

"Damn," I say. "Well, I guess we can stay in touch, emailing and texting."

"Yeah." He frowns, looking troubled.

"What is it?"

"Your mother would've invited me to stay with her," he says. "She did once, when she was in college and I needed somewhere to crash."

"I have roommates. I don't have space," I say, my heart sinking even further. *Don't ask me for money, don't ask me for money...*

"All right," he says, holding up his hands. "I'll figure something out, don't worry."

I exhale. He's not going to ask for money. Ha, take that Gideon and Terrence and Ironwood and everyone who ever doubted his intentions!

He sighs deeply. "This city is so freaking expensive, you know? I don't know how I'll afford a place."

A niggling sense of foreboding grows in my stomach. "You don't have enough with your architect work? There's no salary?"

"Oh, there is. Just, I went and spent most of it in advance, trying to come here. I came to San Esteban early to see you, and maxed out my credit cards as a result."

Shit, *shit*. Here it comes. I stare at my empty coffee cup, at the melting ice cubes inside the clear plastic. On the outside of the cup, the condensation runs down the sides like tears.

"I don't suppose you could spot me a couple grand, so I can put down a deposit on an apartment?" Uncle Karl asks hopefully.

He talked about my mother. He made me feel like I have family, a sense of history with him. He got me to trust him so damn fast, it's disgusting.

"I think we're done here," I say, standing up.

"What?" He leans back.

"You're asking me for money. Gideon said you would, and I didn't believe him."

"Samantha, no, I'm just in a hard spot, that's all. I didn't think you'd get mad about it. Don't be so sensitive, come on. And don't listen to freaking *Gideon*, of all people."

"The worst part," I say, tears blurring him and the coffee shop and everything around us, "is that you lured me into a false sense of security, a sense of family, by invoking memories of my *mom*. Don't contact me again."

I walk to the door, barely able to keep my tears from falling, and I'm vaguely aware of Hunter following behind me.

When I glance back through the window of the

coffee shop, Karl's still sitting there at our table, looking angrier than I've ever seen him.

Good, he should be mad. But not at me—at himself. Because he could've had a family with me, and instead, he wanted money.

TWENTY

Gideon

It feels wrong to travel to San Esteban and not tell Samantha, but for what I'm about to do, it's better if she's not involved.

I heard about her chat with Karl yesterday. She told me she didn't want to talk about it. The Ironwood report on the interaction was brief, no details, but given Sam's reluctance to talk about it, and Karl's status as a swindling asshole, I can guess their coffee date didn't go well.

I'm not going to tell Samantha that I told her so, because I can also guess that she's crushed. I saw it coming, but she had hopes for family, and Karl's going to keep stringing her along unless someone stops him.

Which leads me to this evening's task.

It's only for Samantha that I would meet with this

snake. Otherwise, I'd live my life happily pretending he never existed.

Clay, my driver, drops me off in front of Abdul's. I've been here a couple of times before, with Jaxon and Ryder. It's a decent joint in Dorado Heights. I chose it tonight because it's somewhat familiar territory, and I don't think there's a risk of Samantha showing up.

I'm here before Karl—and that's on purpose. I'm forty-five minutes early. I wanted to choose the table, get my bearings. I order a whiskey and get comfortable in a booth, facing the door. I'm not worried about this meeting, but every good business person knows that being early gets you the advantage.

Karl shows up fifteen minutes after me, probably hoping for the same early advantage, but I was expecting that. I wave him down. Seeing me, he comes over to my table.

"Nice joint," Karl says, looking around as he takes his seat.

"Don't get too comfortable," I tell him.

Something like desperation sparks in his hazel eyes, clings to the bristles of his mustache. Frowning, he says, "What? You invited me here. At least buy me a drink."

I nod at a passing server, who stops and asks us what we'd like. "I'm good, thanks," I say, pointing to my nearly-full glass of whiskey.

"I'll have a gin and tonic," Karl says.

The server takes off. Karl and I face each other.

"So, how've you been?" Karl asks.

"Fine," I say. "Busy. You?"

"Oh, the same," he says with a self-deprecating little laugh.

Running a finger along the rim of my tumbler, I say, "So what's the gig this time? A sweetheart con? Some kind of business deal to bilk entrepreneurs?"

"I have a job, Woodhouse, and a good one."

The server brings over his drink. Once they're gone, I say, "Right. A good job. Are you working as Karl Jeffries, or are you Karl Griffiths for this 'good job'?"

"For fuck's sake." He picks up his gin and tonic and downs it in one go. Grimacing, he sets down the empty glass. "What do you want, Gideon?"

I take my wallet from my jacket pocket and pull out a check. It's already written out to Karl's current alias—Karl Griffiths. I slide it across the table to him, face-down. "What I want," I say, "is for you to go away. Leave Samantha alone, never bother her again."

"So this is fuck-off money?" he asks, giving me a skeptical look.

"Yep."

"It better be a lot," he says, picking up the check. His eyes get huge. "Yeah, okay. She must be worth a lot to you."

"She is." I pull a second check from my wallet and hold it up so he can see it's written for an identical amount. "What you're holding is half of what I'll give you. The rest, you'll get when you're far, far away and can confirm your location."

He laughs in disbelief. "Are you being for real right now?"

"Yeah. I want you gone."

He takes one more look at the check in his hand, and the check that I hold, and he nods. "Consider me gone."

Samantha

Since meeting with Uncle Karl on Sunday, I've buried myself in work at the library, and in writing. I don't want to think about Uncle Karl, I don't want to talk about him, I don't want to remember he exists.

At the same time, I want to call him up and ask if my mother would've fallen for that bullshit he tried to give me.

My understanding is that my mom was a smart woman. She wouldn't have listened to him for a second. As soon as he set up tales of the dead family member to gain sympathy and trust, she'd have seen right through it.

I feel so ashamed.

And that's why I'm not thinking about it, and why my texts back to Gideon and Terrence are brief, why I'm not accepting their phone calls, and why I'm putting off dates with them. Because as much as I want to see them, I don't want to see the pity on their faces.

Then, because I'm apparently not feeling shitty enough, the universe decides to give me the motherfucking cold to end all colds.

"Do you *have* to keep coughing?" Addison shouts at me from the couch in the living room.

It's Thursday evening, and I've been holed up in my bedroom since yesterday, even calling in sick to the library.

"Sorry," I say, but it ends in more coughing. I take a sip of lukewarm tea and wonder if I'm strong enough to get myself a fresh cup.

Nope, I'm not up for a trip to the kitchen. Why have hot tea when there's a perfectly disgusting lukewarm cup right next to me? Millie brought me this tea, dropping it off at my apartment doorstep with a little note saying *Get well soon!* with a cute drawing of a balloon bouquet. It was sweet of her to do that, and even though the tea tastes like something fished from the garbage, I make a mental note to thank her when I go back to work.

My coughing has been so bad, trying for sleep seems futile. Between yesterday and today I've binge-watched an entire vampire television series, and as my finger hovers over the little button to start the spin-off series, I pause. I'm falling behind on the Alex and Calliope story. I was smart and didn't put that shit up for preorder, but if I don't publish, I don't earn money.

And if I don't earn money, I have to either keep on living with crappy roommates, or dip into the allowance Gideon's given me, and nope. I can't live with either of those options.

So, writing sexy times it is, despite not feeling sexy at all.

Alex and Calliope have fucked in his apartment, so far. Now, they need somewhere shiny and new. Maybe I should put them outdoors. A nature preserve, perhaps? She can run from him, and he can chase her. Catch her. Ravish her against a tree.

Everything I wrote, up until recently, was poorly-disguised Gideon fanfiction.

Now I have new inspiration: Terrence.

And I don't know how to choose between them.

MFM books are a thing...can I pull that off? Not gonna lie—I've thought about trying it before, especially after seeing Olivia living a real-life HEA with Jaxon and Ryder.

There's a knock on the door, and I'm pulled away from the paradise of my fictional quandaries. Dammit. Now I remember that I'm sick and feel half-dead.

Addison gives a loud huff of frustration and pauses her show. A moment later, she says, "Samantha, it's for you."

"Tell whoever it is to go away," I say, punctuating my order by blowing my nose. I'm not expecting a visitor. Whoever's guarding me right now must have vetted them, so it isn't Karl. But I feel like shit, and I don't want to talk to anyone. Feeling crankier than I was before, I toss my dirty tissue at the wastebasket. It misses. I leave it on the floor, because if I feel like being a slob, well, I'm going to be a slob.

"Samantha, we're coming in," Gideon's voice calls.

Aw, crap. "Who's *we*?"

"I'm here, too," Terrence says.

Their footsteps get louder as they move down the hall. Addison turns her show back on, but I notice the volume is quieter. She probably wants to eavesdrop. She probably wants to steal these boyfriends like she stole Greg.

Hell, I would too, if I were her.

She can try, but it'll never work. These guys are a million times more honorable than Greg could even *hope* to be.

Right now, they're honorable pains in my ass, because they're showing up here when I look like death warmed over, but whatever.

They appear in my doorway, Gideon in front, and Terrence looking at me over his shoulder. Their faces are tight with concern.

"I'm not up for visitors," I say, sounding just as annoyed as I feel.

"We're not here to visit," Gideon says.

Terrence speaks up. "We're here to take care of you."

I take in their handsome faces and kind eyes, and burst into tears.

"Oh, Sam," Gideon says, rushing forward.

As soon as he comes into the room, there's space for Terrence to stand next to him. Terrence is holding a plastic bag with a heavenly scent coming from it. Gideon's holding a canvas bag. It's hard to tell while I'm crying, but I think there are flower blossoms poking out the top.

Terrence leans over and kisses the top of my head. "I'm going to put this in a bowl for you—I'll be right back."

While he's gone, Gideon unpacks his canvas bag. Flowers, already in a little vase which he fills with water from the bathroom tap. Two boxes of herbal tea —one to soothe the throat, one to help boost immunity. Several packs of cough drops in different flavors. And—

"Harry!" I gasp, hurrying to wipe away my tears.

He holds out the plush hippo, smiling in relief. "You remember him."

"You gave him to me the first time I was sick, after I moved in with you." I take the hippo from him and cradle it in my arms.

"It was Carolina's idea," he says, sounding uncomfortable. "I didn't have a paternal bone in my body."

Funny, I think, *because when we bone, I want to call you "daddy."*

I smile at my unspoken joke and bury my face against Harry the hippo. "Thank you for bringing Harry. And all this other stuff, too. I love the flowers."

Terrence comes into the room, bearing a bowl and spoon. He sets them on my nightstand.

"Chicken soup, with a little extra turmeric and ginger. The deli near my house sells it, and it's what I get when I'm under the weather."

"Thank you," I say, dipping the spoon into the soup and taking a bite. The soup is flavorful and is exactly what I needed.

There isn't enough space to really hang out and I don't have chairs in my room except at my desk. I don't want the guys to leave, though. I feel sick and sad, and even though a large part of me wants to push everyone away...it's too nice having them here.

I scoot to the middle of my bed and pat either side of me. "Do you guys want to stay for a little while?"

They look at what I'm offering, then at each other, and then back to me.

"Sure," Terrence says, settling down next to me on one side.

Gideon takes the other side.

Is this what it's like to be Olivia? She has two hot guys with her—two hot guys that she *loves*—pretty much all the time. The three of them hang out as a unit. They got married, for fuck's sake. I've been happy for her. A tiny bit envious, thinking about the crazy awesome sex they must have.

For the first time, though, I'm getting more of a glimpse of what it might feel like to have two guys united in their goal of making my life better. They're here to support me.

"How did you know I was sick?" I ask.

"I found out through work," Terrence says.

"I called the library, hoping to get in touch with you since you weren't answering my calls," Gideon says.

"I'm sorry, I just..." Karl's face flashes in my mind. The way it transformed from kind and helpful to angry.

"You didn't want to talk about Karl," Gideon says softly.

"No."

"How about a movie?" Terrence asks. "If you get sleepy, you can conk out."

"That's rude, when I have guests."

"We're not guests," Gideon says. "We're helping you, it's different. It's okay to fall asleep."

For some reason, I want to argue with him, but I don't have the energy for it. So I give an imperious wave toward my laptop. Gideon grabs it from my desk and we set it up on the bed so we can all see. I quickly click away from my work-in-progress. At some point, I should tell Terrence about my writing, but that's loaded information. I've never told a boyfriend before, not even Greg, and I got a whole-ass apartment with him.

But I do feel bad keeping it from Terrence, for

some reason. Maybe because Gideon knows, and Terrence doesn't.

We watch a movie. I finish my soup. I'm so cozy and warm, and I'm coughing less than I was. Maybe I could sleep?

Gideon's shoulder looks comfortable, from the way he's sitting. I want to lean on him, but will that make Terrence feel left out, since he's sitting on the other side of me?

"Are you sleepy?" Terrence asks, probably because he sees me eyeing Gideon's shoulder. "You can lean on one of us, and it can be Gideon. I don't mind, baby. Really."

He holds my hand in his, and I take that as permission to rest my head on Gideon.

Maybe these guys were fighting over me in the library last week, but they sure seem okay together now. I wonder what happened to change that. I'm not wondering for long, though, because within seconds, I'm asleep.

I'm not sure what time it is when I wake up, but my room is dark and I'm snuggled against Terrence's side. The guys are talking quietly, their voices low and rumbly and comforting as they seep into my foggy, sleepy brain.

"I have to get back to work," Gideon says. "You can stay with her?"

"Yeah. I don't have work until eleven tomorrow, and I can take a sick day if I need to."

"You guys," I mumble, "it's just a cold."

"You have a fever," Terrence says. "One of us should stay to take care of you, because your roommates aren't."

"It's not their job," I say. "We don't like each other."

"Even more reason one of us should be here," Gideon says. "You need people who care about you when you're sick."

He may have a point. Between the soup, the flowers, the teas and cough drops, and their warm bodies in my bed, I'm getting the rest and care I didn't know I needed.

Why can't we be together like this, all the time? I wonder what they would say if I asked, but this isn't the right time to bring it up. They only just started getting along...I should enjoy this, for now.

TWENTY-ONE

Terrence

When Samantha wakes up the next morning, she looks a lot healthier. I knew the deli's soup would do the trick. That shit's like a magic potion.

Samantha snuggles against my side. One of her legs rests over my hips. Sometime in the middle of the night after Gideon left, I stripped out of my jeans so I'm just wearing boxers and a t-shirt.

"Terrence," she whispers, her eyes still closed. "Are you awake?"

"Yeah." I touch her forehead. She no longer feels too warm.

"I had the best dream." She moves her leg up and down, and her thigh rubs against my semi-hard dick.

My cock swells hopefully. I want nothing more

than to pull her on top of me and watch her ride me. It would be a fucking fantastic way to start the day.

"What was your dream about?" I ask.

"Let me show you?"

Gently, I ease her leg off of me and sigh. "We can't mess around right now, baby—you're recovering from your cold. You should rest."

"I am so turned on, I could die," she says, pouting at me. "If you don't take care of me, *I'll* do it. Please?"

Well, how the hell can I resist her when she asks so nicely? But I'm not fucking her—she's sick, and whatever I want to do with her won't be gentle. So I ease onto my side and push her onto her back. Sliding up her shirt, I reveal her gorgeous breasts with her nipples that are already coming to hard points in the cool morning air.

Leaning over, I take one in my mouth.

Samantha moans and grabs my hand, trying to bring it to her sleep shorts. I don't let her have it. She's not the one in charge here, despite her begging. Instead of fingering her, I lavish attention on her nipple, sucking and scraping my teeth over it, licking at her sweet, soft skin.

"Please, Terrence, please, Sir."

I pull back a little. "Fuck, you're beautiful when you beg."

She moves her own hand to her shorts, but I catch it in my own and hold it above her head. I grab her other hand and do the same. Holding her wrists firmly,

I continue sucking her nipple. After a few minutes, she's practically sobbing with need, begging me to get her off, promising me she'll be good, she won't ask for anything ever again, she just needs to come.

I've probably tortured her long enough. She was sick yesterday, after all. So I push my hand into her shorts, into her panties, and feel her slippery wet pussy. I find the nub of her clit and rub in circles, slowly increasing my speed as I go.

"Right there, oh, fuck, Terrence, Sir, yes," she says. "Yes, just like—oh..."

Samantha comes with a gasp.

While she's still shuddering, I continue fingering her, keeping my teeth and tongue on her nipple. I know I can bring her another orgasm.

A male voice says, "One of your roommates let me in—"

The door opens. The voice that was behind it cuts off and I pull away from Samantha, covering her tits with her shirt in the same motion, protecting her from whoever's burst in.

"What the fuck, man?" Gideon says from the doorway. He's holding a bag with a bakery label on it. "I thought we were taking care of her, not fucking her while she's ill."

Samantha

I sit up slowly, still weak from my orgasm. Now *that* was just what the doctor ordered.

Gideon's frown, however, is not part of my prescription.

"I gave her what she wanted." Terrence gets out of my bed and pulls on his jeans. "Back the fuck off."

Gideon looks like some kind of avenging angel, ready to smite Terrence for daring to touch me.

"He didn't start this," I say. "I started it."

Gideon just shakes his head. "I thought we were on the same page."

"*We*, meaning...?" I prompt.

"All of us." But his glare seems pointed at Terrence.

"You guys need to get over it," I say.

They continue to stare at each other, like each one could vaporize the other with his eyes.

My heart hurts at the sight of it. Yesterday, they were with me together, and it had been perfect. A guy on each side. Am I being greedy? Would I ever have thought Olivia was greedy for having two boyfriends?

Her situation—Jaxon and Ryder—is different, I remind myself. Jaxon and Ryder were already friends, and they'd shared before. Terrence and Gideon just met. And from the way things are looking right now, they don't have any interest in sharing. Talking about it, fantasizing about it, sure. But actually doing it...nope.

Does this mean I'm going to have to choose between them?

Although if they kill each other, which looks likely given the way they're glaring, that would remove my choice entirely, wouldn't it?

I don't want to choose between them. I don't want them to fight.

A part of me wants to just call an end to this whole entire thing. I could go back to what I was doing before—taking home a random guy, and let's be honest, probably a bartender.

The thought is causing my heart to ache. If I don't send them off right now, I'm going to say things I regret.

"You know what?" I say. "Never mind about getting over it. I need some space, you two need space. Let's cool off and figure out what we really want."

"I want you," Gideon says.

"So do I," Terrence adds.

"And I want you both," I say. "Is that too much to ask?"

They glare at each other, not answering. Which is answer enough for me.

"Okay, both of you—out," I say.

Gideon, jaw tight, nods. "I'll go. First—the chocolate croissants are to celebrate. Ironwood just sent me a message that Karl is gone. They tailed him out of town this morning. He's not coming back."

"So we can call off Ironwood's protection," I say.

Terrence holds up a hand. "There's the matter of your room being ransacked. Do we know that Karl did it?"

"Either he did, or he didn't," I say. "How many people, ever, have hired twenty-four-hour bodyguard protection just because their bedroom was broken into?"

Terrence looks like he's going to argue, but then his shoulders fall slightly.

Gideon says, "You can hardly blame us for wanting to protect you."

"I don't blame you at all," I say, "but it's unnecessary now. Karl is gone."

I'm glad Karl is gone, but at the same time, disappointed. Obviously, I wanted him to leave. I just wish things could've been different, that he could've been a real uncle to me, someone to reminisce about stories from my past—stories that, because of not having a family, I lost. So it's not Karl I'm mourning, but my family.

"Okay, here's what's going to happen," I say. "You guys are both going to leave my apartment. You'll cancel the bodyguard service. I want my life back, I'm tired of feeling watched all the time."

"You love being watched," Gideon says with a wink.

Normally I'd laugh, but this is not the right time.

"No more bodyguards, no more monitoring. And I need some space to think about"—I wave my hands between the three of us—"all this."

"Are you calling it quits with us?" Terrence asks.

"No," I say. "I don't *think* I am, anyway. I don't…I don't know what to do. I'm not sure what's the right move. So, time. Space. Can you guys do that?"

They nod, both of them looking solemn.

I stand up and give Gideon a hug, and then Terrence. Then I watch them make their way down the hall and out the door.

Greg is sitting on the sofa, watching a sports channel. He doesn't say anything as Terrence and Gideon leave, but once they're gone he looks up at me, a snide expression on his face.

"Two boyfriends?" he says. "Really?"

I open my mouth to say something catty, but instead of finding a good comeback, I can feel tears forming in my eyes. I purse my lips and open my eyes wide, trying to keep the tears in. Nope, not working.

Greg jumps up. "Shit, Samantha, I'm sorry, I'm an asshole."

"Yeah, you are," I say, holding up a hand to discourage him from getting close to me. With my other hand, I wipe away my tears. "I'm going back to bed."

Samantha

Izzie looks relieved to see me at work. "I thought you would take another day off," she says.

"I'm bored, and I'm pretty sure I'm not contagious anymore," I say. "I even slept last night, so yay."

She cants her head to the side. "Is something wrong?"

"Boy drama," I say. "I don't want to talk about it."

"Okay. Let's go out to lunch today, and we can not talk about it but at least eat something yummy."

"Sounds good. Invite Millie?"

She frowns. "I would, but she hasn't come in yet. She said she'd be late, but didn't give an ETA. I think she's having boy drama, too."

"Well, if she comes in, we should definitely all go out to lunch and *not* talk about our boy drama."

I'm still working on the cataloging and tagging project, so that occupies me for the better part of the morning. Millie shows up about an hour after I did, and she gets straight to work, her eyes red-rimmed like she's been crying. I hear Izzie talking to her from the other room, though, and Millie sounds like she's cheering up.

At lunch, we don't have anyone else to cover the front desk, so we order food in, instead of going out. We get a pizza from the place down the street and take it to the break room. If a patron needs help with something, Izzie or I can see the circulation desk from here.

"Thanks again for the tea you brought over," I tell Millie as we chow down.

Her somber face brightens. "Oh, you're welcome. Did you like it?"

"Uhhh..."

She laughs. "I don't like it, either, but my boyfriend swears by it."

I wait for her to get sad again from mentioning him because of whatever boy troubles have been bothering her, but she seems fine. Maybe she and her guy have already worked things out. That's lucky. I wish my problem was so easy.

It could be, if Terrence and Gideon would just...I don't know. Join forces. Tag-team me. Stop being so damned stubborn.

I've just wiped my greasy hands on a napkin when my phone buzzes. Addison's name shows on the screen, and it's a call, not a text. She always texts.

Immediately, I know something is wrong. A snide, petty part of me wants to let it go to voicemail. But whatever arguments we have, she used to be my friend.

"I have to take this," I say to Izzie and Millie.

They nod and wave their hands, telling me to go ahead.

I answer the call and get up from the table at the same time. Stepping out of the break room, I say, "Addison?"

"Yeah, there's—" Her voice is too muffled for me to hear her words. "It's—bad, I don't know—there's—"

"I can't hear you," I say.

"Sorry it's just—fire—"

A siren sounds from her end of the call, blocking off everything else she's saying.

"Addison?" I say, louder. "Addison, I can't hear you."

"There's been a fire," she says, breathing heavily. It's quieter on her end, now, like she's gotten into a car or something. "Half our apartment is torched. You need to come—you need to come right now."

The phone goes dead. I go back to the table in the break room and look at Izzie and Millie, unable to speak for a long moment.

"What is it, Samantha?" Izzie asks. "What happened?"

"I—my apartment just...burned down, I guess? I don't know, Addison was frantic."

"Go," Izzie says. "I mean, obviously, don't go in unless the firefighters clear it. But go, see what needs to be done. Shit." She looks at her watch. "I wish I could go with you, but one of us has to be at the Corbin."

"I'll go," Millie says. "I can take the time off, I won't be missed."

"It's not necessary—" I begin.

"It's a good idea," Izzie says. "I'll comp you the time, Millie. Thank you."

Millie insists on driving, saying I'm too emotional. I don't feel emotional—I feel kind of blank inside, actually. Maybe the news hasn't hit me yet.

My con artist uncle tried to get money out of me, I had to send away my bickering boyfriends, and now my apartment caught fire. Too many bad things have happened. I want to hide under my bed...but it's probably nothing but ash.

TWENTY-TWO

Terrence

I go home, bolt down a couple of protein bars and some coffee. Put on fresh clothes. I hate removing Samantha's scent, but maybe it's best to try to put her from my mind for a while.

After that, I head to the Ironwood building early. There, I work out for a couple of hours and shower.

One process after another.

Everything's a process, a routine. There's safety in that. Some comfort, too.

Except for one thing: something's wrong. It's a gut feeling. It nags at me when I work out, when I shower in the gym's locker room, when I get dressed for work.

The problem isn't only that Samantha kicked Gideon and me out of her place. It's not only that she wants some space. I don't like either of those things, but they're not the cause of my unease. The problem is something else.

What the fuck is wrong? I feel like I'm forgetting something. Like I left my house unlocked, although I can remember locking the door. If I cooked breakfast, I'd be worried that the burner was left on. Am I forgetting something for work?

I check my schedule on my phone. I'm right where I'm supposed to be. I have to meet with Jaxon and Ryder, but that's in twenty minutes.

I mentally run through everything that's been going on. Jaxon and Ryder's wedding, and their recent return from Hawaii. Nothing is off with that. Val Braggno's death, which is tragic, but was ultimately beyond my control or influence. And then there's Samantha's bodyguard detail, recently canceled. So I shouldn't be worried about that. But...it's something there. Something with Samantha.

Impulsively, I leave the locker room and head down to the tech division. The offices are one floor down, so I take the stairs.

I try Leonie's office first, but she's out. Lin's office is the next one over, and her door is open. I peer inside, knocking on the door frame.

She looks up from her desk and grins, then goes back to typing. "Hey, Terrence."

"Hey." I hesitate next to the chair in front of her desk.

"Uh, you can sit down, you know," she says. "You

don't need an invite. I'm almost done transcribing this report, and I can listen and copy my notes at the same time."

"Yeah. Um." I pause. I don't know how to say it.

She stops typing and looks up at me. "What's up?"

"Probably nothing." I rub the back of my neck, uncomfortable. "Just a feeling."

"I think it's important to listen to feelings."

"I sound paranoid."

"It's only paranoid if it isn't true." The beauty mark at the corner of her mouth lifts when she smiles. "Why don't I check on whatever it is you obviously want me to check on?"

"Fine, thanks. Karl Jeffries."

She scowls. "That asshole. Yeah. He skipped town."

"Is there any way you can verify that he's really gone? This is that paranoid feeling."

"Leonie was handling all of that. She should be back in an hour or so—do you want me to ask her to look into it?"

I check my watch—I'm due for that meeting with Ryder and Jaxon soon. "Yeah, that would be great. Let me know?"

"I will."

"It's probably nothing," I say.

Nodding, she says, "Probably. But it's never bad to listen to your gut."

Gideon

Leaving San Esteban—and Samantha—was the last thing I wanted to do. She had a point, though, that she needs space to figure out what she wants. And that space is probably good for all of us.

It's like coming up with a marketing plan for a client. We complete the plan. All of the elements are there—the creative, the ad copy, the platforms, the budget. But we don't pass it along to the client right away. We wait a few days. Let it sit on its own, without touching it. Then we come back to it fresh.

Invariably, we'll discover at least half a dozen elements that need to be tweaked. Sometimes this is due to our own oversights. Sometimes it's due to a change in the information, or a change in the client's needs. Sometimes it's simply a new direction we come up with now that we're looking at it with fresh eyes.

This relationship, or rather, relationships, plural, between Samantha and me, and between Samantha and Terrence, could use that kind of space.

By late afternoon, that space is benefiting me. If my choice is between not being with Samantha, and sharing Samantha with Terrence, well, I'll share her. I'll do whatever it takes to be with this woman.

My phone buzzes with an incoming call. I'm

hoping for Samantha, but when I look at the screen I see Terrence's name.

So much for space.

I answer the call.

"Gideon," he says. "I had a gut feeling and I asked Ironwood to track down Jeffries again."

"And?"

"Could be that he's just gone underground, but he's unaccounted for."

"He should be gone. I paid him off," I say.

"You what?"

"I gave him a fuckton of money to disappear."

"So you think this is that?" he asks. "Him disappearing?"

"Could be." I drum my fingers over the edge of my desk. "What do you think—will Sam object to another bodyguard detail while we find out where he's hiding?"

"She'll definitely object."

"I think so, too." Fuck. "I'd feel better if I knew where he was, and if Samantha was being watched by Ironwood's people. But let's get in touch with her before we send a detail out."

"I've been trying to call her," he says. "She's not picking up, or responding to texts."

Stubborn girl. "She did say she wanted space."

"Yeah."

"I'm bothered by this. Tell you what, I'm coming back to San Esteban. I'm two hours away. Let's both keep calling her, see if we can convince her to accept a bodyguard for a few more days until we locate Jeffries again."

"We don't actually know that he's a physical threat," Terrence reminds me.

"I don't trust him. Not even for a second. I gave him a lot of money, but guys like him? Sometimes they see that as an invitation to go in for more."

"You think you misjudged him?" Terrence asks.

"It's possible. Fuck, I don't know. We shouldn't have left her today."

"I agree. But she wanted some time to think."

"Yeah."

We're quiet for a moment.

"You said before, we could let her decide," he says. "Let's say she doesn't want to decide. She doesn't want to choose."

I shrug. "Then that's a choice of its own, isn't it? She dates us both, fucks us both, hell, I don't care. Whatever makes her happy, that's what I'll do."

"So we'll both be her boyfriends," Terrence says slowly.

"Yeah. Not like Jaxon and Ryder are with Olivia—that's different."

"They all live together," he says. "We're not doing that."

"No, we're not."

We're quiet again. I don't know what he's thinking about, but I'm thinking about what it would be like if we *were* like Jaxon and Ryder with Olivia. And it doesn't sound all that bad.

"Terrence," I say.

"Yeah?"

"The Karl thing. Keep me posted, will you?"

"I will."

The call ends and I stare blankly around my too-quiet office in this too-quiet house.

Samantha

Millie and I have to park a few blocks away from the apartment building because of all the emergency vehicles clogging the street. We walk toward the building in silence. I'm afraid that if I open my mouth, I'll throw up. How did this happen? And how bad is it? Did the whole building come down? Did I lose everything?

At least I have my laptop, with all of my projects on it. Most of my files are backed up in the cloud, but I would've been frantic about having missed something.

When we finally reach the complex, I exhale loudly. The building is still standing. Maybe the fire happened somewhere else in the building, and all I have to deal with is smoke damage. It's a horrible thing to wish, because it probably means a neighbor would bear more of the brunt of the damage.

Maybe it was a false alarm, and all of our apartments are fine, just fine.

As we get closer, my hopes begin to fade. Soot licks the side of the building—right where my apartment is located.

Millie flags down a firefighter. "Excuse me, but she lives here—can you tell us what's going on?"

The firefighter nods and sticks her helmet under her arm. "The fire's out. We're checking the building, making sure it's stable."

"Do you know how my apartment is? I'm in 2C."

"I don't know, sorry. We need to check that there's no structural damage, first."

"Do you know how long it'll take?" I ask.

"It takes as long as it takes," she says, giving me a regretful smile. "I wish I could be more specific, but... that's just how it goes."

"We understand," Millie says. "We'll wait right here. Thank you."

We wait around, sitting on the curb until my ass goes numb.

"Is there anything I can do?" Millie asks, checking me over with her wide blue eyes. "Anything you need? You know what, I'll be right back—I'll get us some water. Do you want to eat?"

"No, I'm not hungry," I say faintly, staring at my sodden, soot-black apartment window.

She comes back with water and a bag of chips, which she mostly eats while offering it to me periodically. I have no appetite, but I do drink the water.

Finally, the firefighter returns and says, "The building's been cleared. You can go up to your apartment now. But—you said it's 2C, right? It's all wet, smoky. There's damage to the walls. You're not going to want to stay there for a while."

"Shit," I grumble.

Maybe she's wrong. Like, it could be that the damage isn't as bad as she's saying. Perhaps she has really high standards. My standards aren't that high, despite growing up in Gideon's giant house.

"It's going to be okay," Millie says, her voice reassuring. "Should we go check it out?"

"Grab whatever valuables aren't ruined," the firefighter says. "If you need a bag or clothes or anything else, check with Cory at the blue truck around the corner. He has spare items for people who might need them after the fire."

"Thank you," I say, as Millie leads me along.

There's still a crowd gathered, a mixture of people from my apartment complex and curious onlookers. A news van has arrived, but I'm careful to stay out of its way. The last thing I want to do is bare my heart on the local news.

"Samantha!" Addison's voice cuts through the murmuring crowd and she hurries toward me, her brown hair with its pink and purple streaks up in a messy ponytail. "I've been looking for you."

I take my phone from my pocket. "You didn't call."

"My phone died. Damn, can you believe this? I can't believe it."

"Have you been inside yet?" I ask.

"No, is it okay to go in?"

"It is now, yeah." I point to the front doors of the building, where a couple of uniformed officers are checking IDs to make sure only building residents are going in.

Addison scratches at the irritated skin around her nose piercing. "Yeah, let's go."

I'd rather be alone for this—I don't want Addison here, or Millie. But it's Addison's apartment, too. And I can't come up with a graceful way to ask Millie to stay outside. The uniforms see she's with me and let her in.

Everything looks normal in the building at first. I don't even see water on the floor. But I do smell smoke and burnt things. As we get closer to my apartment, the scents get stronger.

Our door is open, and we peer inside. Everything's wet. There are ashy footprints all over the floor from firefighters coming in and saving the place.

"They said the fire started in the apartment next to ours," Addison says quietly. "Right next to your room, Samantha."

Blindly, I walk down the hallway toward my room. It isn't a hollowed-out cavern of ash and rubble, but there's a lot of damage. I can see through the wall to the apartment next door.

My bed is intact, and my dresser, but my desk is destroyed. All of my writing books, gone. Thank goodness I brought my laptop to work with me today, and it's safe in my messenger bag.

The stench of smoke and burning metal pricks my nose. Tears come to my eyes as I survey the ruined bedroom.

"Oh, Samantha, I'm so sorry," Millie says, putting a hand on my shoulder. The contact is maternal, comforting.

"It's just stuff," I say, my voice hollow like a robot's. Most of my sentimental belongings are stored at Gideon's place in Clear Springs. I kept meaning to bring them down here to San Esteban, but that would've meant going up to see Gideon, and up until recently, I didn't want to see Gideon at all.

Score one for spite and grudge-holding.

"You're coming to stay with me," Millie says. "I'll take you there now. I have a little place, two bedrooms. It's nice and quiet. You'll stay as long as you want."

"I couldn't impose—"

"It's not an imposition when I'm offering." She gives me a kind smile. "Can I help you gather whatever you want to save?"

"No, I got it," I say.

While I decide what to bring, she moves things around, scooting the intact items away from the fire damaged wall. Addison's in her and Greg's room, grabbing clothes and throwing them into bags, from the sound of it.

My closet is in decent condition, although everything reeks like smoke. I pull my suitcase from it and load it up with clothes from the dresser, an extra pair of shoes, some toiletries.

"That *asshole!*" comes a shout from Addison's room.

"What?" I shout back. "What is it?"

"He has a whole other tablet hidden in his dresser," she says, thundering down the hall to my room and holding up the device. Her cheeks are blotchy red with rage.

The screen is lit up, and apparently there was no password set, because it's unlocked and there's a photo of Greg with some other woman. And they don't have clothes on.

"Oh, put that away," I say, blocking it from my eyes. "I don't want to see that."

"Well, neither do I," Addison says, her voice choked with angry sobs. "How...how could he do this? There are more! There's fucking *video* on here. Oh god oh god...they're doing it in *my bed*."

Ignoring her, I continue loading up my suitcase, as much as I can. Millie goes to the kitchen, keeping her gaze averted from Addison and the tablet o' cheating. I feel bad for Addison, I really do, but there's a lot of karma at work here.

Millie returns with some heavy-duty plastic

garbage bags. "Let's put everything you want to wash in these," she says. "I don't have a washer at home, but I can either take you to a laundromat or store them for you until you want to deal with them."

"Thank you, that's smart," I say.

Continuing to ignore Addison, who's gasping and crying while she flips through more and more images on Greg's secret tablet, Millie and I load the bags with my remaining clothes. Hopefully the smoke stench can be washed out.

Finally, we finish. There's nothing left to do.

I take a bag in one hand, my suitcase in the other. Millie takes the other two bags. I glance over at Addison. "I guess we're off. Good luck."

"That's it?" Addison says. "That's all? You're not going to, I don't know, support me? He *cheated* on me, Samantha! You, of all people, should know what this feels like."

Yeah, I know what it feels like, because she and Greg did it to me.

"Oh, there's one thing left," I say.

She looks at me hopefully.

I walk past her to my bed and grab Harry the hippo, tucking him under an arm so I can still carry my suitcase and garbage bag.

Then I leave.

TWENTY-THREE

Samantha

Millie's car is an older-model sedan manufactured before the time of dashboard screens and phone plug-ins.

"The CD player is broken," she says with an apologetic smile. "Radio okay?"

"Sure." We've left San Esteban behind, and we're on the freeway going west. It took us so long to get into my apartment—hours, and then it took time to pack, so now the sun is hovering just above the horizon. The glare through Millie's dusty windshield is intense. Shielding my eyes from the worst of it, I say, "Um, where do you live?"

"Fair Heights," she says.

"Oh, I didn't realize you live out of town."

She laughs a little. "I mean, it's just a suburb, it's

not that far away from San Esteban. I don't mind the commute. The city's so expensive, ya know?"

"Yeah, I know." Here I was dragging my feet on moving out, leaving my roommates behind, and now I've been burned out of the apartment, instead. It's all for the best, but I hope to hell that my publishing income can continue to grow.

We drive for some time, and Millie pulls off the freeway and onto a frontage road. We follow it for a few miles. The trees are getting thicker here where there isn't farmland. I'm surprised by how remote it's getting. Fair Heights is a suburb, not a tiny town.

I pull out my phone—I should probably check in with Gideon and Terrence. When I told them I needed space, I hadn't been planning on leaving town to get away from them. I might pull up a map, too, see exactly where we are.

There's no reception, though, and I can't even bring up the internet.

"Millie, when you said your place was quiet, did you mean it's literally out in the middle of nowhere? I'm not even getting reception."

"Oh, don't worry," she says. "You can't get reception here, but once we get to my place, I have wifi and you'll be able to make calls and check messages and all that."

"And...just how far away is your place?" I ask.

"It's close." She shoots me another reassuring smile.

I am not reassured.

Up until this morning, I had twenty-four-hour bodyguard protection. It wasn't for no reason at all, but we thought the threat gone.

What if the threat isn't gone?

"Really, I don't mind all the driving, if that's what you're worried about," Millie says.

No, that's not what I'm worried about. But I just give her a smile that is probably more of a grimace. The frontage road has veered away from the freeway, and I haven't seen any other cars in a few minutes. My inner alarm bells are clanging.

"I imagine, with how your parents died, you're not a huge fan of traveling of any kind. But trust me, I'm a great driver."

My parents died in a helicopter crash. But I don't talk to anyone about how they died. Not even Izzie knows how they died.

What exactly does Millie know, and how does she know it?

Clearing my throat, I say, "Yeah. It's just it's so unpredictable. Nobody would've seen the runaway train coming."

"Runaway train?" Her nose scrunches up. "I thought it was a helicopter crash?"

She shouldn't know this. Our names were kept out of the news. Nobody talked about it—not Gideon, not me, not the attorneys. If she was cyber-stalking me, it would still be impossible to find.

Gideon, me, and the attorneys weren't the only people who knew, though.

There was one other person: Uncle Karl knew.

"Millie," I say slowly, "yes, it was a helicopter crash. Who told you that? I didn't tell you."

"Oh." She waves her hand like it's no big deal. "Izzie mentioned it in passing, the other day."

"Izzie doesn't know, either."

She huffs a sigh. "Okay. Fine. I guess I may as well tell you. I know your uncle."

"Karl?"

"Yeah. He's a good guy."

Anger and disbelief are making it hard to breathe. Shaking my head, I say, "This isn't okay. None of this is okay. I want to go back to the city, right the fuck now."

"There's no need to be upset," she says.

"No need? You've been lying to me this whole time! When did you meet him? Did you know him before—" I break off, because this sounds paranoid. But I have to ask. "Did you know him before you got the job at The Corbin?"

"Yes. I know it sounds bad, but it isn't."

"Millie, this is *bad*. So bad. He's trying to get money from me!"

"Because he needs it," she snaps, her blue eyes flashing with anger before softening. "He lost his whole family, and he needs money."

"Now it sounds like he's conning you, too," I say.

"He just wants to talk to you! He's gone to great

lengths to get you here, and so have I," Millie says, shaking her head. She must be in denial, like she's so far into this con, she believes it, too. "Please, you have to trust me."

"He just wants to talk to me...and he's gone to great lengths? What do you mean about 'great lengths'? The apartment fire...wait. The apartment fire, too?"

She nods. "We made sure nobody would get hurt. It was all under control."

This is...this is insane. My hands are clammy and cold. I need to get away from her. Right the fuck now. She's taking me right to Karl, and he couldn't get money from me by asking. Is he going to use force?

"Let me out of the car," I say. "Now. I'll walk back to San Esteban."

"No, please—"

I reach for the handle.

"Don't, Samantha," she says. "You'll get hurt—I'm not slowing down. Stay in the car!"

She's too busy watching me. I'm not watching the road, either. I'm staring out of my window, looking for a good place to jump out of the car. There isn't much— just a ditch running between the road and the trees. If I do this, I'll have to hope Millie slows down a little more.

"Stop the car," I tell her. "Do it now, or I'll jump."

I go to unbuckle my seatbelt, and Millie reaches over to stop me.

The car swerves.

My seatbelt locks me into place as we veer to the other side of the road.

Millie overcorrects and we spin.

There's a deafening *crunch* as the nose of the car slams into the ditch. My head flings forward, but the airbags deploy. I squeeze my eyes shut. I feel like I got punched in the face, and then again in the chest where my seatbelt restrained me.

When I open my eyes again, Millie is slumped back in her seat, her airbag deflated in front of her. Blood trickles from her nose.

"Millie?" I whisper. I shake her shoulder.

She moans, but she doesn't open her eyes.

The car has dipped into the ditch, but thankfully we're mostly upright. I find my phone on the floorboards, where it slipped to the front. I check for service, but there's nothing, no reception. Shit.

I unbuckle my seatbelt and take a deep breath, rubbing the sore spot between my breasts where the belt caught me. Carefully, I check to see if my door will open. It isn't easy, but I shove against it with my shoulder and it finally springs free.

I grab my purse and my bag with my laptop and clamber out of the car. I should probably try to pull Millie out, too, right? Or isn't it that if someone moves, their spine could snap or something? Should I wait? I need to get help.

I climb out of the ditch, holding onto the car's side for leverage. Then I'm up on the frontage road.

The sun has finally descended below the horizon and its light is fading quickly. Visibility is poor, and there's no shoulder on the road to speak of. If there were a lot of traffic, or any traffic at all, I'd be worried about getting hit.

But there's nothing. Nobody.

I go to the driver's side of the car and look into the shadows and gloom of the ditch. "Millie?"

A pained moan comes from the car.

"I'm going to go get help, okay?" I say.

"Oh…okay. It's just so dark."

I hate leaving her, even though this whole shitshow is her damned fault.

Sighing, I clamber and slide back into the ditch. I hate not being able to decide things like this, but what if the car explodes or something? I figure it's not likely, but I would never forgive myself if I started walking and then Millie died, trapped inside of a burning car.

Having an active imagination sucks sometimes.

"All right, hold tight," I say. "Do you think your spine is broken or anything?"

"No, I can move everything. It just…ugh. Wait. I can get out, actually. I just unbuckled. Can you open my door?"

It's jammed against a rock and some soil, but I dig that away from the car door and yank it open.

Millie's frightened eyes meet mine. "I'm surprised you're not running away."

"I'm not a dick," I say, holding a hand out to help her out of the car.

"Well, I appreciate that."

"So how far away—really—is your place?" I ask.

"A few more miles." She takes my hand and winces as I pull her up and out of the ditch.

"Can we walk to it?"

She looks up and down the road and shrugs. "I guess we're going to have to. I just...whoa. I need to sit down for a second."

I try to ease her down, but she falls heavily to her ass, right there on the road.

Her eyes water and her face scrunches in pain. "I don't think I'll be walking anywhere right now," she says. "My head's spinning."

"Okay," I say. "Okay, um, all right. I can go find someone. You just hang tight. But maybe out of the road, okay?"

She scoots back.

I can't believe I'm helping get her to safety after she, what, kidnapped me? Maybe "kidnap" is too harsh, but she got me to come with her under false pretenses.

I'm angry one second, and pitying her the next. I don't have the energy for this emotional rollercoaster, so I shove all my feelings down and start walking.

Gideon

When I get to San Esteban, I go straight to Ironwood. I'm ushered into the building and shown to a large room with a giant table. A dozen people are working at computers and looking at tablets, sharing things with each other, speaking in low voices. It's not chaos—this company is too professional for that. Rather, it's a concentrated energy, a busy hum, as everyone in this room works on locating Samantha.

"This is the tech and cyber investigations department," Jaxon says.

"And the plan is?"

"Find your girl," Ryder says. He claps me on the shoulder before moving over to a pair of workers who are absorbed with a computer screen. A quick glance shows me they're checking traffic cam footage. I don't know how they got access to it, and I don't care to ask. Whatever little bit helps us, I'll take it, even if it's not entirely legal.

"It could be she's perfectly fine and lying low for a bit," Jaxon says.

Terrence shakes his head. "She's not with her roommates, her boss, or Olivia. She's not answering her phone when I call or text, not when Gideon calls or texts, and not for Olivia, either."

Jaxon shoots him a look. "Before I was interrupted, I was going to say those same things."

He takes Terrence aside and their lowered voices

are barely audible to me, just bits and pieces of their conversation. I hear "emotional involvement" and "trust our process" and "we haven't lost anyone yet."

"Except for Cal," Terrence says with a glare.

I wonder who Cal is. That Ironwood has lost him, or anyone, doesn't inspire confidence.

Rather than tell Terrence to stand down, Jaxon just gives a sad shake of his head and points him in my direction.

"So she's gone," I say.

"We're trying to find out where she would've gone, and who with."

"There was a fire at her apartment building," he says.

My heart jams my throat. "Fuck. A fire? Was she there?"

"She should've been at work when it happened. We're trying to track down her boss, but she isn't answering her phone."

A woman with a long, gray braid stands up and motions to Jaxon, urgently trying to get his attention. I hurry toward her, as well.

"I just got off the phone with her supervisor at The Corbin," the woman says.

Jaxon nods. "What's the story there?"

"According to the supervisor, Samantha got a phone call about her apartment fire, and she rushed over to the building."

"But her car is still at The Corbin," someone else at

the table says.

"Yes," the gray-haired woman says. "The supervisor told me that another employee, Millie Sorento, gave Samantha a ride to the apartment building. After that, she doesn't know what happened to Samantha."

"What's the damage to the apartment building?" I ask.

"According to the fire station, some units are destroyed. Others are fine, but smoke- or water-damaged," one of the tech people says.

If her place was damaged or destroyed, Samantha would need a place to stay. It would make more sense for her to come to my place, or to Olivia's, but if the solution were standing in front of her, offering, she might have gone with someone else.

"Did Samantha's supervisor give you Millie's address?" I ask. "Maybe Samantha went home with Millie, if Sam's apartment isn't livable."

"She should've called someone—one of us—to let us know where she was going," Terrence says, looking like he wants to hit something.

"Maybe," I say. "Maybe not."

If he and I hadn't been arguing over her, she wouldn't have taken a break from us, and she'd likely be staying with me or him right now. We would've been her first phone call.

"Leonie, we need Millie's address and phone number," Ryder says.

"Done," she says, handing him a slip of paper. "Do

you want me to call her?"

"Yes," he says, and Leonie starts dialing.

A moment later, she says, "No dial tone, it goes straight to voicemail."

"Okay, I need a team to go out to Millie's place," Ryder announces.

Terrence starts for the door. I follow quickly behind him, along with Ryder and a couple of other Ironwood people.

"She lives out in Fair Heights," Leonie says. "I'll text you all the address."

She doesn't text me, but that's okay, because I'm following Terrence out of the office and into the parking garage below.

He doesn't even ask me, just gestures with his chin toward one of the black Ironwood SUVs. I climb into the passenger seat and he gets behind the wheel. Seconds later, we're peeling out, and a Fair Heights address is on the navigation screen in the dash.

A second SUV is behind us with the other Ironwood people.

"If she's not with this Millie person, where could she be?" I ask. "We can't rule out Karl."

"Half of the office is working on locating Karl," Terrence says.

That's good, but it's not good enough. This shouldn't have happened. We should never have let our guard down.

Fuck. *Fuck.*

TWENTY-FOUR

Samantha

I don't know how long I've been walking. My feet are killing me, though, because I'm wearing impractical work flats. I thought I'd be sitting at a desk in The Corbin for most of the day. Instead, well, I get this.

I'm not even mad anymore. I've walked long enough, I can almost understand what's going on with Karl. For whatever reason, he's in dire straits. He probably didn't want to engineer this whole thing, but he didn't feel he had a choice.

Every few minutes, I pull out my phone and search for reception. Every time, there's nothing. I go longer and longer between breaks to check. Just how far did we drive, anyway? I'm walking back toward San Esteban, because I don't know how to get to Millie's, and I figure in this remote area, it's better to head toward what I know than not.

The sound of the car reaches my ears. I perk up, hopeful. The noise grows louder. It's coming from behind me, so I turn around. The headlights illuminate the road, blinding me.

I wave the car down. I must look like a crazy person, wildly flailing in the darkness, but Millie needs help, and so do I.

The car slows. Thank goodness. My shoulders relax in relief.

The driver rolls down their window and a familiar voice says, "Samantha, thank God you're okay. I've been worried sick about you and Millie."

I blink, still seeing spots from the headlights' glare. Vaguely, I can make out the shape of his mustache and slowly, the rest of his face. "Karl?"

"Yes, it's me."

"Where's Millie?" I ask. "Did you pass her and the car?"

"She's in the back seat, unconscious. I'll take her to the hospital after you and I make our arrangements."

"Arrangements?"

"You must know I need money," he says, his voice amused, yet also chiding.

"You've been setting this all up," I say slowly.

"Well, yes. Not the car accident, but Millie will be fine when I drop her off at an ER."

He's so cavalier about it. I bet he isn't even going to

stay with her. I'd thought I wasn't angry. I thought, a few minutes ago, that I had reached some understanding. But seeing him here in a very shiny car, with a smug expression on his face, and juxtaposing that with my aching feet, my stomach twisted in knots, and a giant headache from that stupid airbag deploying in my stupid face...my blood pulses hot in my veins and I want to rip his head off his shoulders. He's the reason I'm here, in pain, walking for over an hour in stupid shoes. He's the reason my apartment burned. He's the reason behind all of this.

"You organized this *entire* thing," I shout, pointing at him.

His smug expression transforms. His hazel eyes, barely visible in the darkness, are full of chilling rage.

"Get in the fucking car," he snarls. "I didn't do this for nothing."

I think I'm finally seeing my uncle as he really is. An angry, selfish, conniving man. And there's no way I'm getting in the car with him.

When I hesitate, he holds up a gun. The click of the safety coming off is louder than the car engine, louder than the frantic thudding of my heart. I hold up my hands. "Okay. Okay, I'm getting in the car."

It's a two-door sports car, so I have to go around the front to get into the passenger's seat. I peer in the back window to see if Millie's okay.

The back seat is empty.

He didn't even pick her up? He just...left her by

the side of the road? Fury coats my vision, followed by fear. I knew he was a liar, but now he's holding a gun. And if I get into this car, I might never get out alive. He'll take what he wants, and then kill me.

So I run. Straight into the woods at the side of the road. My bags bang into my sides with each step, but I don't stop to shrug them off. All I can do is move forward.

"Samantha! Get back here!"

A shot sounds, and I scream. There's no pain—I don't think a bullet hit me.

I stop running. I crouch down into a little ball and hide behind a tree, tucking my bag and purse nearby. Here I am in the woods, hiding. My brain takes me back to the nature preserve, when I'd run from Terrence. But then, I wasn't really trying to get away. Then, I wanted to be caught.

Here? Now? No, I can't be caught. If he catches me, I don't know what he's going to do.

"Samantha," he calls.

I don't respond.

"Look, just transfer the money over, and I'll get out of your hair." Karl chuckles. "I have my phone ready, and I have reception. I just need your code, sweetheart, that's all."

Ew, he called me *sweetheart*.

Folding my arms across my chest, I shake my head. I'm not answering him. I'm not going to have anything to do with him.

"Samantha? Where are you? Don't make me come into the woods to find you. I'll be very cranky. Just tell me your banking information.

"Answer me, dammit!" Karl says.

Wait, he said he has reception? When was the last time I checked my phone?

It's a risk to pull out my phone—the screen light could give Karl my location. But I need someone to know where I am.

There's a single bar of reception. I don't know what street this is, some unnamed road, but I'm able to grab the coordinates from my maps app. Hunching over my phone to hopefully block out its light from Karl's eyes, I share the coordinates with both Gideon and Terrence.

I don't know what Karl is doing. Did he see the light from my phone? I shut it off quickly. It's already on silent, so that's good.

Holding my breath, I listen. The woods are quiet, and there's no wind to rustle the trees

The woods grow lighter so quickly I know it can't be the sunrise. Someone's here—Gideon and Terrence? How could they have reached me so quickly? There are sounds of car doors opening, and someone shouts, "Drop your weapon! Right now, right fucking now!"

It's Terrence's voice, sounding mean and scary and protective and oh my God if we get out of this, I'm going to kiss him so hard, hug him, and tell him how much I care. Gideon, too. Whatever bullshit is happening with them not wanting to share time with me, we'll get through it, I know we will.

"I said drop it!" Terrence shouts again.

Please, please let him be okay. Let him be safe.

There's the sound of more cars approaching, and the woods get even brighter.

"Okay, okay, I'm dropping it," Karl says.

I stand up slowly. My legs are shaking. I need to get out there, to see that Terrence is okay, that Karl is finally defeated.

A gunshot sounds.

"No!" I scream, and bolt for the road.

Stupid. I know. I can't make myself stop, though.

A second gunshot.

I reach the side of the road. I crawl back through the ditch. Terrence is standing up, his arms low, a gun held loosely in his hand. Gideon is right behind him, also holding a weapon.

Rocking back and forth on the ground and cradling one arm with the other is my uncle. "You shot me," he yells, spittle flying from his mouth. "I can't believe—"

"You tried to shoot Terrence," Gideon says, while Terrence takes big strides toward Karl and kicks Karl's weapon away.

Terrence looks to the side and sees me. "Samantha."

"How'd you get here so fast?" I ask.

"We were already on our way," Gideon says. "After talking to Izzie, we thought maybe you'd gone with

Millie. The coordinates you sent were the confirmation we needed."

As we speak, everyone who has been still and watching bursts into a frenzy of activity. Ryder is here, and several other people from Ironwood. I babble about the car accident, and Millie, and point down the road where she's still probably waiting, hopefully unharmed. Just because she was in on Karl's plans doesn't mean she deserves to die. And I have a feeling he duped her just like he tried to dupe me.

I hate feeling like a fool, and that's what he made me, what he made Millie.

"She was complicit without even realizing she was a victim," I say.

"We'll get her," Ryder says, motioning toward some of the Ironwood people.

I hold tight to one of Terrence's hands and one of Gideon's. Neither of them pulls away, which is good, because I couldn't handle that kind of rejection right now.

Someone from Ironwood goes into the woods for my bags and hands them to Gideon because I refuse to let the men go. Someone else wraps up Karl's arm, then muscles him into one of their SUVs. Karl shouts incoherent nonsense, mostly about what a bitch I am and how selfish it is for me to just sit on all this money. He calls me a poor little rich girl.

"That's it—we're leaving," Gideon says. "Terrence?"

"Yeah, let's go." He gets Ryder's attention and points to one of the big SUVs.

Ryder nods and says, "Samantha, please give Olivia a call. She's worried sick."

"Okay." It's the middle of the night, but I call her anyway, while Gideon and Terrence walk me to the car. I tell her everything while I get settled in the back seat. Gideon sits next to me and Terrence starts driving.

The reception is cutting out, so I say goodbye to Olivia and tuck my phone into my bag, exhausted.

Now it's just me and the guys, and I don't want to talk anymore.

They both seem to realize this. Gideon wraps an arm around my shoulders and tucks me against his side, and I'm asleep in less than a minute.

Terrence

"Where to?" I ask. "I can drive us up to Clear Springs. Free gas, on Ironwood's dime."

Gideon's voice is quiet so he doesn't disturb Samantha. "I think she'd rather stay in San Esteban. She mentioned wanting to get together with Olivia in the next couple of days. If she wants to be in Clear Springs instead, I'll come down for her in a heartbeat."

And he would. Just like I would. We both care about this woman so fucking much.

We don't speak much as I drive us back to San Esteban. I don't go back to Ironwood to return the car, but drive straight to my place. Samantha's fast asleep even when I stop the car. I open her door and ease her out, picking her up.

She wakes as I carry her up my front steps.

"It's okay," Gideon says from just behind me. "We're taking you to Terrence's."

Her eyes flutter shut again.

"You can stay over," I tell him as we go inside. "It's not a mansion or anything, but the couch is comfortable enough."

"We should've gone to my place," he grumbles, his green eyes narrowing, but he doesn't look too upset.

He follows me into my room, where we get Samantha's shoes off. Her legs are scratched up from when she was in the trees, probably. I hate to wake her, but we need to clean the cuts. Gideon helps her sit on the edge of the bed, her long legs dangling down, while I get a couple of washcloths.

"Sorry, baby," I say, cleaning the scratches with the soapy towel while Gideon wipes the soap away with a wet one. I want to murder Karl for putting Samantha through this, and then I want to dig him up and murder him a couple more times. Fucking asshole, hurting our girl.

Our girl. Huh.

"It's okay," she says, her eyes half-closed. "Barely stings."

"You're going to be safe here," Gideon says, kissing her forehead. "I'll see you soon."

She grabs his wrist and tugs him down for a second kiss, which he gives her on the lips while he eases her back until she's lying against a pillow.

My heart clenches—not with jealousy or envy, but with affection for Samantha.

I see Gideon out. The three of us will need to figure out a way to make this work. I can't give Samantha up, and I wouldn't want to see her give up the love she obviously has for Gideon, either. And it would be a crime to keep her from him when he loves her so much in return.

Samantha

When I wake up, I'm alone in Terrence's bed. Where is he? I touch the spot next to me. The sheets and pillow are cool. Didn't he sleep here? And where's Gideon—I thought I heard them talking last night, but I wasn't sure if Gideon stayed or not.

I remember Gideon kissing me goodnight.

I want that every night.

Whoa, where did that thought come from? I shouldn't want that, should I?

Well, I can't really think on the shoulds and should-nots, because I probably shouldn't have fucked my dad's best friend, but we did that. And I hope sometime to do it again.

Great, now I'm turned on and I'm alone in Terrence's bed.

I'm wearing a shirt and bra, and panties. At some point during the night, I kicked off my pants.

Well, since I'm in my underwear and no one's around, how freaky would it be for me to take care of myself? I mean, it wouldn't be the freakiest thing I've done.

I listen hard. The house is silent. I should get up and go look for Terrence. Why take care of myself when I can ask him to satisfy me?

But first, I can't resist rubbing my thighs together. If I do it just right, I can almost make myself come.

I close my eyes and imagine Terrence is here. Gideon, too. They're both in this bed with me, their masculine scents surrounding me, their hands warm against my skin.

"Samantha?"

Terrence's voice startles me, and I freeze.

He steps into the room. His voice sounds amused as he says, "Open your eyes, baby, I know you're awake."

Shit. I crack open one eyelid and peer at him through it.

"What are you doing?" he asks.

"Nothing." I clear my throat and sit up. My horniness is very much still present, but I try to speak past it. "What happened with my things? Millie had helped me get a bunch of stuff from my apartment."

"We got your bags of clothes and other items from the back of Millie's car. We even found your hippo. Henry?"

"Harry."

"Harry, we got him." His brown eyes scrutinize me as he comes to the edge of the bed and sits down. "Are your legs hurting you? They were all scratched up, and just now you were moving them a lot. Do you need some ibuprofen? Some other pain med?"

While I scramble to come up with an answer, a million lies flash through my mind. My ankle was itching. I was dreaming about running. A spider got in the sheets and I was trying to smash it with my knees.

Then Terrence starts laughing. He throws his head back and his deep, resounding laugh fills the room.

While I stare at him, completely confused, he leans over me and smiles. "If you're wanting to get fucked, baby, all you have to do is ask."

I'm mortified, but not so mortified I can't ask for what I want. "I want to get fucked," I whisper.

He nods, looking satisfied. Big old jerk.

But instead of getting naked, which is obviously the next, logical step, he passes me my phone from the nightstand.

"Call Gideon."

"What?" I ask.

"Call him. Right now. Tell him I'm here. Tell him you want him to talk to you like he did that time I overheard everything."

"You overheard...?"

"You and him, having phone sex in your apartment. Yeah, I shouldn't have listened, but I did, and now I want to *watch*."

My mind whirls. He was listening that day? Fuck, that's a turn-on, too. But this is...this is too kinky, right?

I trace the edge of my phone on the bedspread. "I don't think—"

"Do it."

TWENTY-FIVE

Terrence

Her expression, a mixture of lust and "oh no, I shouldn't do this," is a gorgeous thing to behold.

My cock started getting hard as soon as I saw her wriggling around in my bed. I had a pretty good idea of what she was doing, but her guilty expression when I caught her only solidified that idea into knowledge.

I had thought she'd be too wiped out for sex—emotionally and physically—after everything that happened yesterday.

On that count, I was wrong, and I couldn't be happier.

"Are you going to call Gideon, or do I need to dole out some spankings?" I ask.

She blinks at me. "Both?"

Leaning down, I kiss her lips, her cheeks, her chin, then I nuzzle my way down to her neck. Against her skin, I say, "Call him, or I'll punish you, and I don't think you'll like it. It won't be spankings—it'll be keeping you from that orgasm you seem to want so bad."

"Okay, calling him now." She reaches for her phone, then hesitates.

"Are you nervous?" I ask.

"A little." She gives me a brief smile, takes a deep breath, and taps her phone screen.

The phone's up to her ear, and I ease her shirt up, touching the soft skin of her belly, moving my hand toward one of her breasts. Her soft intake of breath is cut short when Gideon answers, his voice just loud enough for me to make out the word. "Samantha."

"Hi," Samantha breathes.

"Hey, precious girl. How are you feeling?"

"I'm—good. Um, really good."

"Tell him I'm here," I say, pinching her nipple.

She squeaks. "Terrence is with me." A pause while Gideon speaks too quietly for me to hear, then, "Yes, we're in bed together. Kind of. He's sitting next to me." She pauses again. "He wanted me to call you. I don't think I need anything, no."

"You do need something," I tell her, giving her another light pinch.

"What was that?" Gideon's voice is a little louder on his end.

I whisper in Samantha's ear, "Put him on speaker."

She taps her phone screen and says, "You're on speaker now."

"Gideon," I say.

"Terrence. I was just asking Samantha if she needs something." His voice is casual, like this is an everyday kind of conversation and I'm not sitting here with my hand up his girlfriend's shirt.

"She does need something, but she needs to tell you what it is," I say.

He waits. I wait. Samantha bites her lip and her thighs flex subtly under the sheets; I can feel the slight movement next to me.

"I want to come," Samantha says.

"But you don't need it?" Gideon asks.

"Um...I need it," she admits. "Really bad. Really, really bad."

"Bad enough to do everything I say, right now?" he asks.

I grin. This is exactly what I was hoping for—I knew he'd be down for this, the kinky bastard.

"Yeah," Samantha says. "I mean, yes, Sir."

"Good girl. Take off your shirt. Show Terrence your tits."

"He's already touching them," she says.

"Good, now show them off. Your breasts are beautiful, Samantha—you shouldn't hide them from us."

I let go of Samantha's nipple and she lifts her shirt over her head. Underneath is a flimsy little bra of some see-through fabric that has my mouth watering. He's right—she shouldn't hide from us.

I cup her tits, rolling her nipples gently between my fingers. She lets out a little moan.

"Tell me what's happening," Gideon says, his voice sharp.

"He—he's touching my breasts," Samantha says, then gasps. "He's squeezing my nipples a little bit."

"Are you nice and wet?" he asks.

"Yes, Sir."

"Good."

I stop fondling her and lean back against the headboard, curious about what might happen next. Samantha's pout of disappointment is cute, and I kiss the corner of her mouth.

"What's happening now?" Gideon asks.

"He—he stopped touching me," she says.

"You can ask him to resume."

"Terrence, Sir?" she says. "Please touch my breasts?"

"Nah, I'm good here," I say.

She gives me an indignant look, like *get with the program*, but I shrug and smile.

"He won't touch me, Sir," she says toward the phone.

"Hmm, that is a problem," Gideon says. "I'm not there, or I might do it myself. Or maybe I'd make you beg for it. Do you think that's what he wants—for you to beg?"

"Maybe?" Samantha turns to me and says, "Please, Sir? I really, really want you to touch me. Please. I'm crazy for it, crazy for you. Please, I want it so badly. I'll be good for you, I'll do whatever you want. Please?"

I pretend to be unmoved, when in reality, my dick is rock hard. "What's in it for me?"

At first she looks like she wants to throttle me, but then she turns her attention to the phone and says, "What's in it for him, Sir?"

"Well," Gideon says, "I can't be entirely sure. But it sounds to me like you need to get out his cock and suck it, precious girl."

She reaches for the fly of my jeans, but I grab her hand.

"You can't touch without asking," I say.

"Ugh," she exclaims. "Okay, so I was trying to be patient and play along, but now this is just getting ridiculous—"

I flip her over so she's across my lap, facing down. She's wearing panties that match her bra. I leave the panties up and give her three quick spankings.

"Ow, ow!" she shouts.

Once she quiets down, Gideon says, "Samantha, what happened just now?"

"Terrence *spanked* me," she says, trying to squirm off of my legs. "*Rude.*"

I spank her again, partly for good measure, partly because I just like the way her plump ass feels beneath my palm.

"He did it *again*," she says.

"It sounded to me like you deserved it, with that attitude," Gideon says. "Terrence, would you mind giving her three more for me?"

"Gladly." I spank her three more times, enjoying the way my handprint shows up over her pale ass cheeks where her panties don't cover her. When I'm done, I ease her panties down to look at the rest of her ass. "Nice and pink," I say aloud, for Gideon's benefit, before I put her panties back.

"Now," Gideon says over the phone, "Samantha, do you think you can ask Terrence nicely to allow you to suck his cock?"

She turns her head to look at me from her prone position. "Sir, may I please suck your cock?"

It twitches beneath her.

"Yes, you may," I say, like I'm granting her some kind of favor instead of being about to receive a fucking *gift*—Samantha's lips on my cock.

She crawls off of my lap to kneel next to me. Her hands are at my zipper, easing it down, then pulling at my jeans. I help her until my cock is free.

"Are you sucking him off?" Gideon asks.

"Almost," Samantha says. "I'm about to, Sir."

His voice is harsh. "Get to it then, precious girl."

She leans over and takes me in her mouth. I involuntarily flex at the sensation, which pushes me in farther than she anticipated. She gags a little and I immediately pull back.

"Fuck, you're gagging on him?" Gideon says. "Do that again."

I don't want to hurt her, but she seems into it, moaning as she goes down more, harder. She gags again, pulling up and coughing, her beautiful eyes watering.

"Could you hear me, Sir?" she asks, her eyes on mine but obviously speaking to Gideon.

"I did. You're doing a great job. I want you to give Terrence a show now. Give him everything I want. And I want to see you play with your tits while your pussy gets so wet you can see it through your panties."

"Yes, Sir." She falls back on the bed and starts touching her breasts, rolling her nipples.

"Tell me what you're doing," Gideon says. "Everything."

"I'm playing with my tits like you said." Her voice is breathy. "My panties are already wet. I don't know if Terrence can see that or not."

I can. There's a damp spot right over her crotch. "Yes, I can see," I say, crawling toward her. "I need a better look, though. Let me take off those panties, babe."

She lifts her hips and I pull down her underwear, revealing her gorgeous pussy. I'm so close to it, I can't resist giving her a swift lick.

"Yes," I murmur, "nice and wet for me."

"For us," Gideon says, reminding me that he's here, in a way.

And I invited him, for fuck's sake. What was I thinking?

I was thinking this would be hot, and it is.

"Are you still playing with your tits?" Gideon asks.

"Mm-hmm," Samantha answers.

I lick her pussy again and she moans. I delve my tongue into her, wanting more of her taste, wanting her to feel more.

"What else is happening?" he asks.

"Terrence is...oh, fuck, he's eating me out." Samantha writhes on my bed, her legs tight against me. She tastes exquisitely sweet and I lick at her, loving the way she squeezes my head with her thighs until I have to hold her open so I can move.

Gideon's voice is guttural. "Keep talking, precious girl. Tell me everything."

"He's...he's holding my legs apart. He's—oh, fuck. He's sucking—ah—he's sucking on my clit. His tongue is fluttering, or something?"

"Are you still touching your tits?" Gideon asks.

"No, Sir, I forgot...I am now, though."

"Good girl."

Her thighs clench, trying to close around me again, but I keep her legs open with my shoulder and one hand. I bring up my other hand and press a finger into her cunt. She's wet, so fucking wet. I need to fuck her. Not sure how long I can hold out before taking her even further.

"Sir, S*irs*, it feels so good," she says. "Holy shit, it feels amazing—Gideon, I wish you were here, too, oh fuck, oh fuck."

I pull away and sit on the edge of the bed. "Up here, babe," I say, patting my lap.

My cock juts up, and I quickly put on a condom.

"Gideon, Sir, Terrence is putting on a condom," Samantha says. "He's ready for me, and I'm so, so wet. Please don't make me wait."

"Does she deserve your cock, Terrence?" Gideon asks.

"She's been a very good girl," I say. It's twisted. We're veering into some daddy-dominant territory. I'm not against it at all, but I don't know how Samantha's going to respond.

But she kneels here on the bed in front of me, her cheeks and chest flushed with desire, her bra yanked down so her tits are exposed, her pussy slippery wet because that's how I left it. And she smiles.

"I've been so, so very good, haven't I, Sir?" she whispers.

Oh, fuck, I want to come right fucking now.

"Get on my cock, babe."

She swings a leg over me so she's sitting on my lap. "I'm climbing onto Terrence's lap, Sir," she says toward the phone. "His cock is right here, it's so big, and I'm sliding down—ahhh."

I don't know what Gideon's doing on his end, but I

know if I were in his place, I'd be jerking off right now. As it is, I'm here with her, and she's so tight and hot and slippery, she feels so good. It shouldn't be possible to feel this good.

"Talk to me, precious girl," Gideon says, his voice rough.

Yeah, if he's not jacking it, he will be soon.

"Terrence is inside of me. I'm so full. I have to move—I have to."

"Hold still a second," Gideon says. "Savor it. Savor everything."

Samantha's blue eyes meet mine, and she looks a little mischievous. She rocks her hips a tiny bit.

Taking at her, I shake my head and grab one of her nipples between my fingers. I twist it just enough to see her face contort in pain, and she whimpers.

"What's that?" Gideon asks.

"Our girl tried to move anyway, despite what you said," I tell him.

"He hurt my nipple," Samantha says.

"I wish I could see that," Gideon says. "I like it when you hurt, it turns me on."

Samantha's pussy clenches over my cock. I think she likes the idea of being hurt.

"Tell him," I say. "Tell him you like it."

"I like it, Sirs," she whispers. "I like it a lot."

Gideon swears and says, "Then do it again."

I don't take orders from him, but it's a good fucking

idea, so I do it, holding one of Samantha's hips in place with a hand and using my other to abuse her nipple. She moves a little bit, unable to help herself, but I don't mind in the slightest. Every writhing motion, every pained little moan, every squeeze of her cunt on my cock is pushing us toward our inevitable, ecstatic end.

No more of this. I flip her around so she's lying on her back, her knees wrapped around me. I hold her hands above her head. She's stretched out, body open to my gaze. Perfect. A slow drag out, then I push back in, moving in the way that'll rub against her clit as I go.

"Yes," she gasps.

"Tell Gideon what I'm doing to you," I say.

"He's fucking me, Sir," she says.

I pull out, then back in again. It's fucking heaven. "Tell him in detail."

"I'm—I'm on my back," Samantha says, her voice breathy. "He's holding my hands. My legs are wrapped around him. He's fucking me slow, Gideon, Sir. Oh fuck, it's amazing, you should be here."

"Would you like me there sometime?" he asks.

"Yes, oh fuck, oh *fuck*, I'm going to come," she says.

"Thinking about him here with us, that gets you off, doesn't it?" I whisper in her ear. "One of us watching while the other one fucks you. Maybe he'd holding you down while I fuck this pussy. I'll make it mine. Then he takes a turn while *I* hold you."

She cries out, "I'm coming," and her entire body

arches beneath me, showing me. Her cunt rhythmically clenches over me, and her legs tighten around my hips. She fights to get her hands free, but I hold them up, loving that I can keep her where I want her, use her body for my own pleasure.

My slow strokes are no longer slow—I'm pumping fast and hard, taking what I want. She's mine. I'm here with her, nobody else. Gideon can listen all he wants—I'm the one fucking her.

The vicious possessiveness I feel is exactly the kick I need. I smash over the edge, my orgasm spilling out. I kiss, bite, lick, suck every bit of Samantha I can reach with my mouth—her lips, jaw, her neck, oh that sweet neck. She smells so good. I bite down, claiming her, licking over the mark as soon as I let her go.

I want to stay buried in her for hours.

I roll off her, though, not wanting to crush her. She gives me a lazy smile.

"Good?" I ask.

"Incredible," she says. "Let's go again."

"I'm down. Let me deal with the condom."

"Okay. Gideon? Gideon." She leans over to look at her phone. "Dammit. He hung up."

Gideon

I end the call to the sound of Terrence's grunt of satisfaction. But it's Samantha's moans of ecstasy that echo in my mind, her soft voice rising and falling with her pleasure, then her announcement that she's coming, which is the sexiest thing I've ever heard or ever will hear.

Indescribably hot.

The whole interlude was beyond words.

I wipe my come from my chest with some tissue from the nightstand drawer. Then I head to the bathroom to toss the tissue and give myself a more thorough wipe-down.

I'm patting myself dry when the doorbell rings. I don't bother putting my shirt back on because it's probably just a delivery and the driver and truck will be gone by the time I get downstairs.

I pause at the door to Samantha's old bedroom. There's just a hint of her cherry-vanilla scent in the air. I lean against the jamb and breathe it in.

The past few weeks, I've been wondering why I can finally offer Samantha the support and care I should've been giving her all along. Now I think I know what has changed—love.

Or maybe it was that, back then, she was a child, and I was afraid of loving her the way I do now? Not in a sexual way, because I'm not an actual predator. I've never lusted after a minor. But the feelings in my heart, in my soul, are so deep. She was a literal child, too young for the feelings I have for her now that she's an adult.

My brain feels scrambled. I still don't have this figured out. Maybe I never will figure it out.

I am an asshole for not taking proper care of her—there's nothing to be done about that now, though, except make it up to her as much as I can.

What we just did with Terrence, even if it was over the phone and not in person? Maybe that will help repair some of the damage.

The doorbell rings again. Odd. I probably have to sign for the package. I don't want to bother with my app to see who's there, because if the delivery person leaves and I have to make a trip to the post office to pick up whatever it is, I'm going to be pissed.

Opening the door, I freeze. It takes my brain a long moment to catch up with what my eyes are seeing. With *who* my eyes are seeing.

Her brown hair is shorter, a pixie cut that emphasizes her big, hazel eyes and pouty lips.

I can barely find my voice. "Ashley? What the fuck?"

She throws herself into my arms. "Gideon—Gideon, I've missed you so much."

I hug her back automatically, but she feels different in my arms. She doesn't quite fit with me, not like she used to. I'm extra aware that I never put a shirt on, and

I very much wish I had done so, now. It was a mistake. One more mistake in the string of many, it seems.

"Gideon," Ashley says, clinging to me, "tell me you've missed me, too. Tell me we can still get married."

SAMANTHA, Gideon, and Terrence's romance continues in *Dirty Diction*, the second book of the four-book series. It's coming out in January 2023! Find links to retailers at https://calistajayne.com/dirty-diction/

ALSO BY CALISTA JAYNE

Their Little Liar

Filthy Fiction

Dirty Diction

Tempting Tales

Naughty Novels

Their Babydoll

Daddies' Girl

Daddies' Babydoll

Daddies' Little Angel

Daddies' Princess

Daddies' Sweetheart

Daddies Ever After

Cinderella's Daddies

Falling for Them

Kneeling for Them

Submitting to Them

Belonging to Them

Fiercely Filthy Fairy Tales

Little Red's Temptation

Rapunzel's Sweet Release

ABOUT THE AUTHOR

Calista Jayne adores filthy, smutty romances featuring dominant-yet-tender men. When not writing or reading, she's falling in love with the heroes in K-dramas or walking along a California beach.

Join Calista's newsletter to get showered in love notes (also known as newsletters and updates about new releases and sales) and receive a free book. Visit https://calistajayne.com/babydolls-newsletter to sign up!

Printed in Great Britain
by Amazon